After Dinner Conversation Themes
Bioethics Edition
Philosophy | Ethics Short Story Fiction

After Dinner Conversation *Themes* – Bioethics

After Dinner Conversation publishes fictional stories that explore ethical and philosophical questions in an informal manner. The purpose of these stories is to generate thoughtful discussion in an open and easily accessible manner.

ISBN 979-8-9896194-3-6
Library of Congress Control Number: 2023952699

.

Copyright © 2024 After Dinner Conversation
Editor in Chief: *Kolby Granville*
Edition Editor: *Ben Mulvey*
Story Editor: *R.K.H. Ndong*
Copy Editor: *Kate Bocassi*
Cover Design: *Shawn Winchester*

Design, layout, and discussion questions by After Dinner Conversation.

https://www.afterdinnerconversation.com

After Dinner Conversation believes humanity is improved by ethics and morals grounded in philosophical truth and that philosophical truth is discovered through intentional reflection and respectful debate. In order to facilitate that process, we have created a growing series of short stories across genres, a monthly magazine, and two podcasts. These accessible examples of abstract ethical and philosophical ideas are intended to draw out deeper discussions with friends, family, and students.

Table Of Contents

FROM THE EDITION EDITOR .... - 4 -

SACRIFICING MERCY.. - 5 -

THE HUMAN EXPERIENCE.. - 20 -

EUTHANASIA .... - 34 -

IN DEFENSE OF THE HARVEST .... - 45 -

TWO-PERCENTERS... - 56 -

THE DECAY .... - 73 -

VISIONS OF MIDWIVES... - 90 -

ON GOOD AUTHORITY .... - 103 -

STEP BACK.. - 130 -

ALL HARRIET'S PIECES .... - 152 -

AUTHOR INFORMATION.. - 163 -

ADDITIONAL INFORMATION .... - 166 -

* * *

From the Edition Editor

Before there were mechanical respirators the question of when to disconnect a patient from such a machine to allow death to come did not arise. Before dialysis machines became publicly available, the question of who will benefit from this technology and who will we allow to die were not asked. Such hard moral questions were often beyond our capacity to imagine. But imagination is the purview of fiction.

As a professor of philosophy, I am familiar with scores of bioethics textbooks designed to introduce college students or medical professionals to the complexities of ethical decision-making in the biomedical realm. But those textbooks, replete with discussions of ethical theories, usually lacked the intimate details of real lives necessary to connect theoretical insights to the nuances of real moral decision-making, the kinds of judgments that real people must make in often tragic circumstances. So, I would often look to fiction for what I needed.

That brought me to the *After Dinner Conversation* series of stories that directly address ethical issues. The stories gathered together in this volume speak to a broad array of ethical concerns specifically in the biomedical realm. They each represent a cluster of issues and questions that usually appear in bioethics textbooks. But they illustrate real life in ways not found in those textbooks.

All good fiction, all good speculative or science fiction, is interesting if it captures a relatable sense of reality. The stories in this collection can potentially sensitize us to the complexities of the present and reveal images of the about-to-happen, such that we are not completely surprised when it comes time to make the serious moral choices that we inevitably must make.

Ben Mulvey – Editor

Sacrificing Mercy

Henry McFarland

* * *

Inwardly I raged against Jenny's religion, her God, and yes against her. She had a chance at life, at health. How could she refuse it? Damn the religion that told her to destroy our hope! But showing my rage would make it harder to persuade her. Besides, it was time to help her into bed. The doctor's visit had exhausted Jenny, and she quickly dropped off to sleep. She looked as peaceful as a saint in a stained-glass window and as fragile.

On a spring day ten years ago, a petite young woman with a pixie haircut pushed a shopping cart piled high with groceries across our college campus. Some cans fell from the top of the pile. I picked them up and offered to help push the cart. Jenny's bright blue eyes widened in a smile that lit up the world.

Jenny led me to the food pantry at a local church, where an obese woman with a loud cough sat on the stoop and puffed on a cigarette. Jenny sat next to the woman and said in a cheery voice, "Good morning Mrs. Simpson, I hope you feel better.

Come on inside, we've got tomato soup—your favorite."

Mrs. Simpson might have been better off if she used the money she spent on cigarettes to buy her own soup. Still, something in Jenny's kindness to her touched me. Because of that, and to spend time with Jenny, I began to help in the food pantry—just one day a week. Soon my life revolved around Jenny. We married the week after graduation and settled down for a blissful four years of health.

Then came four years of sickness. Cardiomyopathy attacked her heart and began a deterioration that doctors could slow but never stop. I did what I could for her, including learning how to draw her blood for the tests that never found any hope. Nothing stopped the disease. Every halting step she took, every moan she made, every tear she shed reminded me of how helpless I was.

Only a new heart could save her, but the chance of that was slim. People who needed hearts far outnumbered the donors. The hospital put her on a waiting list, but she'd likely die waiting.

My one source of hope was a daily internet search for information on possible new treatments. Three years ago, there was something promising. I told Jenny about it as I drew her blood. "They just started trials on a way to grow a new heart."

"So that's why you looked so intense, like you wanted to jump inside your computer. How could they do that?"

"With stem cells from embryos that are clones of the patient."

Her eyes narrowed. "Cloning's unnatural."

Nature wasn't helping us much. "It's a way to get a new heart without waiting for a donor." I swabbed a spot on her arm with alcohol. Her flesh once had a rosy glow—now it was almost blue. "You'll just feel a little pinch now."

"You're always so gentle. Mike, what happens to the baby?"

"Baby?"

Her eyes got narrower, her forehead wrinkled. "The embryo, what happens to her?"

"Don't know. Maybe they won't have to use an embryo."

As the disease progressed, Jenny's life seemed to shrink. One by one she had to give up the activities she loved. Her worst moment was when the doctor said that she could no longer teach. She wept on our way home after that appointment, and her hands clutched the cross she wore around her neck. At home, we embraced on the sofa, and she poured out her sorrow and frustration.

"I feel so useless."

"Jenny, no, you still mean the world to me."

"I can't work. I can't help around the house. I can't even be a wife to you anymore."

I was all too aware of that last loss, but I didn't want that to show. "You're the woman I love, and don't you ever forget it. You aren't useless."

Jenny hugged me tighter. "I love you too, Mike. I must have faith. God has a reason for all this."

I didn't say anything about God's reasons. Soon after we'd started dating, Jenny gave me her big open smile and asked me to go to church with her that Sunday. At Calvary Evangelical, the congregation gathered in a large undistinguished space with a high ceiling, like the waiting room in a train station but with an altar and pews. Nothing hung on the walls but a large cross.

During the service, she stared at the altar with a wide-eyed fascination. I was mildly interested, or maybe less than mildly. Luckily it only took an hour.

As we left, Jenny gave a little laugh. "At least you didn't fall asleep. That's a start."

Time to be positive. "I liked the choir."

She hugged me. "You're a good person, Mike. Keep coming to church. You'll get it."

I didn't get it. Jenny wanted me to go to church, so I did, but with no real conviction. For hope I looked to research, not to heaven.

* * *

Now research could save us. The trials were over, and the method worked. Dozens of patients had gotten newly grown hearts. Jenny had a chance, and I brought her to Dr. Yifang Phang to take that chance.

The doctor explained the procedure. "All we need now are some cells from your body—a blood sample will do fine. We can use that to start the cloning."

Jenny's voice was weak but clear. "What happens to the baby?"

Dr. Phang took a deep breath. "You mean the blastocyst? It would not be viable after the stem cells were extracted."

"So you'd kill her."

Dr. Phang sounded as if she were reading a script. "Some would feel that way. Others would question whether a blastocyst, that's what I prefer to call an embryo at such an early stage, would really be a baby."

Jenny leaned forward. Her eyes were fixed on Phang. "Whatever you call the embryo, it's a human life at its earliest stage, when it's most helpless, most vulnerable."

"Not all share your point of view. Also, the process here is not similar to the typical process that results in the birth of a baby. The blastocyst would be formed by somatic nuclear cell transfer, not the union of a sperm and egg."

Jenny paused for a moment. "Is there any other way to get the stem cells?"

Phang shook her head. "Not for this procedure. It requires embryonic stem cells because of their greater pluripotency, their ability to become other types of cells. In a few years, we may be able to use other types of stem cells. But Mrs. Thompson, you don't have that time. Without a new heart, you won't live more than a few months."

Jenny sighed. "Could we do something else instead?"

"This new procedure is the only way to get a heart. There's no real chance of an old-fashioned transplant with a donor heart. Now that we've developed this new technology, getting donor organs has gone from hard to almost impossible. No one thinks of donating organs when new organs can be grown instead. Besides insurance wouldn't cover it."

That surprised me. We hadn't had an insurance problem before. "Why not?"

Phang gave me a sympathetic look. "Because the heart wouldn't have the recipient's own genetic makeup, the patient would need lifetime treatment with anti-rejection drugs. Those drugs are very expensive and often have serious side effects. Because it's so much more expensive than using an organ cloned from the patient, the insurance companies won't pay. The cost is well over two million, not including the anti-rejection drugs post-transplant."

That we could never afford.

"Doctor, I can't have this procedure." Jenny sounded so calm.

I reached over and touched her hand. "Jenny, this could save you."

She turned to me. "I'm sorry, Mike. But this procedure is wrong. I can't do it. I don't fear my death."

I feared her death! Without her I'd be alone. I felt nauseous. We'd been on a long journey, and with the destination finally in sight, she refused to move. Phang was the specialist. Couldn't she say something to change Jenny's mind?

Phang's voice showed no emotion. "Then all I can do is continue palliative care. You should sign a living will. Also, you'll need a medical power of attorney. You're likely to go into a coma before you die, and you should designate someone to make decisions for you during that time." She gave us the paperwork, and Jenny left the office with me trailing behind.

The next night, Jenny, her breathing slow and labored, lay in bed. I sat next to her and took her hands in mine. "Please Darling, have the procedure. I need you, to have you near me, to hold you."

Jenny sounded regretful but adamant. "Mike, I love you so much. Please try to understand. The procedure goes against my beliefs."

"If you have this procedure, you can have your life back. You can teach again. Once you told me that poor people shouldn't be denied medical care. How can you deny yourself medical care?"

Jenny began to cry a little. "Mike, I don't want to die. But do you remember in my second year of teaching when that little boy Bryan died of cancer?"

"You cried all night."

"I did, but that taught me that yes, bad things happen, and we don't know why God lets them happen or what his plan is. But we always have God's loving presence in our lives, and that presence gives our lives meaning. To find that meaning, we must follow God's laws. There's no true hope in going against those laws."

I stroked her hand as she dropped off to sleep. Jenny had spoken from an inner strength. Perhaps I should have admired that. I couldn't.

* * *

Jenny's mom came over a couple of days later. Esther Davis was a quiet, diminutive woman in her early fifties. We weren't close, but we got along. Jenny told her mother everything, so Esther knew about her daughter's refusal and its consequences. Esther was as religious as Jenny. What side would she be on?

The three of us sat on the sofa with Jenny in the middle. Esther shook her head no to my offer of tea or soda. She fixed her eyes on her daughter. "Jenny, I've been thinking about the procedure and praying about it, and I believe you should have it."

Jenny's eyes widened. "I've prayed about it too, Mom, and I've talked to the pastor about it. I can't do it."

"Jenny, Jesus says, 'I desire mercy, not sacrifice.' You're only twenty-nine—if you don't have this procedure, there's no other hope."

Jenny reached over and touched her mother's hand. "There is, there's always hope in God."

"Please Jenny," Esther pleaded, "Jesus wouldn't want my baby to die."

"Jesus teaches us that sometimes we must suffer for our faith. The early martyrs knew that."

"What about Mike? You'll be leaving him all alone."

Jenny kept looking at her mother, not at me. "I know it's hard on Mike. I know, but..."

Esther began to sob. "You don't know how hard. You don't know how hard it is to lose the one you married. I'd have done anything to save your father."

Jenny sounded sympathetic but unmoved. "Jesus comforted you when Dad died. Jesus will comfort Mike too."

I kept silent, not saying the comfort I wanted was health for Jenny.

Esther moved closer to her daughter and put her arms around her. "Jenny, you're my only child. Please promise that you'll continue to think about the procedure and pray about it. I love you, and God loves you too. He wants you to live."

Jenny hesitated. "I'll still pray about it. But I have to follow the Lord." She bowed her head for a moment. "I have to rest now, Mom."

Jenny watched through the window as Esther's lonely, stooped figure walked to her car. Then she sighed and went up to bed.

The next evening, Jenny sat next to me on the sofa and took my hand in hers. "Mike, I have to give someone a medical power of attorney. It has to be someone who'll respect my wishes." She stared up at me with big eyes the pale blue of the early morning sky. "Can I trust you to do that?"

We were preparing for when she would slip away from

me and into a coma.

Jenny went on talking. "At first, I planned to ask Mom to do it, but it might be too hard for her. Can you make sure only good things are done?"

I looked her in the eyes. "Yes. Yes I can, and I will." I embraced her and rubbed my hands over her back. I hoped I'd find the courage for what I knew I had to do.

* * *

Dr. Phang and I met in her office, where nothing hung on the walls but her medical degree. She leaned back in her chair. "Mike, growing a new heart takes time. If we're going to do it, we have to start now."

"Jenny's still against it."

Her voice softened. "I'd been hoping that she'd change her mind. But if she won't, we'll have to talk about end-of-life care."

"Suppose you developed a heart from someone else's cells. That would solve the problem of not having a donor heart, wouldn't it?"

"Yes, but the patient would still need anti-rejection drugs, so insurance wouldn't cover it."

I already knew that. "Just growing the heart itself isn't too costly, is it?"

"That alone no, but what's the point of doing that if you can't use the heart?"

"How much would it cost for everything up to the operation?"

She gave me a *why do you want to know that* look. "First there'd be the compatibility tests on the DNA. Those are about $5,000. Then there'd be the growth of the blastocyst, the harvesting of the stem cells, and the growth of the heart. That would be about $25,000."

"Could you postpone the compatibility tests until after the heart is grown? If I can't use it, I don't want to pay for more than necessary."

She hesitated for a moment. "Yes, we could do that. The tests don't take long, and they don't have to be done until just before the operation."

I drew a small vial of blood from my pocket and put it on the desk in front of her. "This is my blood. My wife won't agree to using her cells in cloning, but you can use mine. Grow a new heart from my cells."

"Wouldn't your wife still object—it would involve embryonic stem cells?"

"Maybe she'll change her mind. You make sure that if she does, there's a heart for her."

"What about the cost of the operation and the anti-rejection drugs?"

"My worries, not yours."

She looked at the blood. Then she looked at me the way a TV cop looks at a suspect. "You realize, Mr. Thompson, that the law has serious penalties for using someone's cells in cloning without their permission."

"So what? They're my cells, and you have my permission."

"You're sure?"

I tried to sound irritated, the way someone who was telling the truth would sound. It's especially important to sound truthful when you're lying. "I know when my blood is drawn. If you want me to sign something, I will." I signed a lot of forms and left her with the blood.

Jenny's life faded like a picture left in the desert sun. Eventually, she lapsed into a coma, and they took her to the hospital. Dr. Phang met me in a small conference room near the emergency room. "I'm very sorry about your wife's condition, Mr. Thompson, but we do need to discuss how to care for her."

"Doctor, take the heart grown from the blood sample I gave you and transplant it into her body."

The doctor looked grave. "As the heart was based on your cells, I can't transplant it without first preparing your wife with anti-rejection drugs. That would—"

"You won't need any anti-rejection drugs. That was her blood, and the heart is genetically hers."

"You told me that it was your blood. She didn't authorize using her blood." Her voice showed no emotion.

"What do you care? I told you in writing that it was my blood. You're off the hook, aren't you?" She opened her mouth to speak, but I kept talking. "All that matters now is you have a heart that matches her genetically. I have medical power of attorney, and that gives me the right to make treatment decisions for my wife. I'm making that decision. Give her the cloned heart."

"I have to report the unauthorized cloning."

"Go ahead. You can't be blamed for cloning the heart, and you'll face no consequences for it." I waited a second, then went on. "If my wife dies because you refused her a legally authorized treatment, that'd have consequences."

They let me see Jenny after the surgery. She looked tiny and frail as she lay in a large bed with tubes running into her body and monitor screens all around her. But she lived.

In a few days, Dr. Phang thought Jenny was well enough to be told why a healthy heart now beat inside her. When the doctor finished her explanation, Jenny turned on me. "You knew I didn't want this! You betrayed me."

"Jenny, it was the only way to save you."

"You haven't saved me! Leave me alone now, please." She turned her face to the pillow and began to sob.

Dr. Phang touched my arm and suggested that I leave.

Four days later, her nurse called to say that Jenny wanted to see me.

She sat up in her hospital bed. Color had returned to her cheeks, and her eyes were bright. She was like a flower that was blooming again, but her eyes bored into me. "Mike, I can't accept what you did."

"I needed you to live. I wanted to have you—"

"Yes, you needed, you wanted. You didn't do it for me. You did it for yourself."

"Darling, you wouldn't be alive if I hadn't done it."

"You don't understand. I'd wondered for so long—I knew God has a reason for my suffering, but I didn't know what it was. Finally, I realized that the Lord allowed my sickness to happen because by refusing the treatment, I could show others how wrong the treatment is. My suffering could have had a purpose, but you destroyed that."

Could I make her understand? "Your suffering showed that you needed help, and I got it for you."

Jenny's voice softened. "You didn't help me. My life was based on principles. That's what gave it meaning. Now I must live a life that comes from betraying those principles, a life that's been forced on me. Can you at least tell me you realize what you did was wrong?"

I took a long deep breath. "Saving you wasn't wrong."

Tears began to run down Jenny's cheeks. "Then we can't be together Mike. Please leave now."

* * *

I had to spend only four months in prison, a chance to get a lot of exercise and read a lot of books. The hardest part was knowing that when I'd be released, Jenny wouldn't be there.

One day they brought me up to the visitors' room. Dirt had turned the white walls a light gray, and the air reeked of unwashed flesh. Dozens of voices filled the room with a throbbing sound. Esther sat there braving it all. "Mike, I want to thank you for saving my daughter's life. I told her that Jesus who called Lazarus from the grave would bless what you've done."

"How is Jenny?"

Esther smiled. "She's a lot better. She's going to teach kindergarten this fall."

"That's so great."

Esther's hands moved closer to me. Perhaps she would have hugged me, had prison rules allowed it. "Mike, she feels hard against it now, but I'm praying that Jenny will forgive you and that you and she will reconcile."

"Thank you so much, Esther." How could reconciliation be possible? Jenny would never accept what I'd done. I'd never say it was wrong.

When I was released, they found me a new job and a small apartment. Its bare walls kept saying Jenny wasn't there. One day I walked past her school. The kindergartners were playing in the school yard, and a little boy fell down and began to sniffle. Jenny went to him. She was as quick and light on her feet as before the sickness. She comforted the boy then sent him off to bravely rejoin the game. I didn't let her see me. She wouldn't want her ex-con ex-husband hanging around.

Later I passed a large red brick church and decided to go inside. The church was much more ornate than the one Jenny attended. Sunlight streamed through stained-glass windows and filled the space with color. I knelt before a mural of a robed figure with long hair and a beard and prayed to the God who had called Lazarus from the grave.

* * *

This story first appeared in the After Dinner Conversation—October 2020 issue.

Discussion Questions

1. Do you respect Jenny's decision to refuse treatment? Would you refuse treatment if you were in her shoes? Is your opinion different, knowing that the blastocyst that would be destroyed would be just a few hundred cells?

2. Is Jenny being selfish to others by refusing treatment based on her religious values? Would she be selfish if her religious values caused her to refuse more common treatment, like a blood transfusion, or taking antibiotics?

3. Even if the husband disagreed with Jenny's decision, did he have a duty to honor her wishes? Did Jenny have a duty to divorce him after she found out what he had done?

4. Is a person's sense of honor, duty, and/or faith more important than their life? Is a person's first duty always to their life? Why or why not?

5. Jenny says, *"I realized that the Lord allowed my sickness to happen because by refusing the treatment, I could show others how wrong the treatment is. My suffering could have had a purpose, but you destroyed that."* Is Jenny correct, given that she didn't personally accept treatment? Does it matter that, even if she died, practically no one would have known she refused treatment, or is the symbolism of the refusal the important thing?

* * *

The Human Experience

Jared Cappel

* * *

Always make them wait. Couples love to talk, young ones especially. We're not allowed to record them, but there are no laws on amplifying. Our waiting area is designed to project their voices, magnifying their speech and feeding it directly into my earpiece.

It's important to get a good look at them too. The wife, Morgan, is clearly on edge. She walks around the room, studying every fold in the wall, like a dog sniffing around the perimeter of her yard. Her husband, Thad, sinks into a chair, a pile of pamphlets in his hands. He flips through them, rolling his eyes, tossing them aside. One final pamphlet catches his eye—a list of packages with a detailed breakdown. This wasn't on the website.

Morgan seems nervous; Thad, angry. This is important to know. Morgan controls their general discourse, but Thad likely has the final say. His tone is rather gruff, insisting. When he speaks, his wife listens. When she speaks, which is often, he barely acknowledges her, refusing to lift his eyes from the pamphlets.

I make them wait another ten minutes before letting them into my office. I've gathered all the intel I'm likely to obtain, but the longer they wait, the more the power shifts into my hand. A simple tactic, and a rather understated one at that, but it's effective. We have the data to prove it.

The couple is much friendlier to me than they were to each other. They shake my hand, accept some coffee, settle into the chairs across the desk from mine. Morgan begins rambling off all the information she's learned about our process. Some of the statements are posed as questions but, really, she's just trying to impress how much she knows. It's clear she's read a lot into this. I rate her understanding of our procedures in the upper range.

Thad is still focused on the pamphlet in his hand. The details in the pamphlet are a bit different than on the website. This is intentional, though there's no way for him to know that. He becomes rather specific and accusatory with his questions. His voice remains gruff; his words, deservedly paranoid. His understanding of our procedures isn't quite to the level of his wife's, but his distrusting nature is rather astute.

I smile to let them know their concerns are heard, and I pull a form from the second drawer of my desk. "Before we get into all that, have you decided which package you are thinking of purchasing?"

"The gold," Morgan says, "though we'd consider the platinum if you can talk us into it."

"Honey, we discussed this." Thad hands me a stack of papers. "We qualified for a loan for the gold package. We really can't afford anything higher."

I give the documents a perfunctory glance and begin to fill out some information on my form. "This all appears in order. We do have other financing options available for the platinum package, but we'll get to that in good time."

Morgan leans forward in her chair, lowers her voice to a whisper. "Is it really true that the platinum package is the highest?"

"Yes. It's been written into law."

"Well yeah, we know that, but surely royalty and such aren't locked into such restrictions like us plebeians."

"I can assure you they are."

"I don't believe it."

Thad nudges his wife and signals for her to be quiet. "She's just an employee, dear. If there's anything shady going on, she wouldn't know the half of it." He smiles at me. "No offense, of course."

There's nothing he can say that would really offend me, but his assumption of my naïveté certainly works in my favor. Any issues he raises can be deflected to the company. "None taken," I say, "but I am quite confident no one can go above platinum. The entire process is codified, made public, and reviewed for irregularities."

"We've read the website," Morgan says, then stops herself. "Sorry, you must take me for quite the shrew."

"It's okay. All hopeful parents just want what's best."

"Or second best in our case," Thad says with a smile, but his wife isn't laughing. He continues. "Please tell us more about the gold package."

"The gold package entitles you to one hundred and fifty additional attribute points, which you can give to your unborn child across any or all of the eight domains—physical health, mental health, attractiveness, intelligence, likability, athleticism, confidence, and our newest attribute luck."

"Luck?"

"Yes, if you place your points on luck, the attributes will be spread at random across the domains."

Morgan laughs. "Can you imagine that, honey? Leaving all this to chance... like barbarians!"

Thad doesn't quite catch his wife's comment, his attention lost deep in the folds of the pamphlet with the divergent information. "It says here with the gold package, we start with fifty points in each domain?"

"Not quite," I explain. "You get fifty points for both physical and mental health, meaning your child will be born with average genetic makeup in these domains. In the other domains, your child starts out at twenty-five, meaning they're at the twenty-fifth percentile."

"So below average."

"Yes, in a sense, but you have one hundred and fifty other points to play with. If you want to do things conservatively, you could spread the points evenly across the six lower domains, and your child's genes will be perfectly average."

"Average?" Thad asks. "This is an awfully expensive way to end up with an average child, don't you think? Seems like mother nature could do that herself."

"But can she guarantee it?"

Thad slinks back into his chair and stuffs the pamphlet into the breast pocket of his jacket.

"Or you can place the points on the attributes that are most important to you," I say.

"What attributes do most parents go for?" Morgan asks.

"For many years, physical health was our top seller, but it's since been passed by mental health. Many parents realize there's not much to life without happiness."

"So our child can be happy as long as it's ugly and dimwitted?"

I summon a line from my script. "I really think you're underscoring just how many points you have to play with. Why don't you use the attribute bars on the monitors to see how much freedom you really have?"

I swivel two monitors in front of the hopeful young parents-to-be. They each take their own approach to building the perfect child. Thad focuses on intelligence, athleticism, and health, jacking up the points in these attributes at the expense of the others. Morgan is more conservative with her choices, trying to make sure her prospective child doesn't lag in any one area.

Morgan scowls at her husband. "So you want a child with no confidence?"

"It'll be confident because of how damn capable it is."

"Uh huh, all people with a 28-likability score are brimming with confidence. People love to be loathed."

"Well, at least the child I created can use its intelligence to excel. What is your average Jane going to accomplish in life? You need talents to get ahead. You can't get anywhere sludging through the middle."

"My child will be healthy, intelligent, and reasonably capable. What more can we ask for?"

"Greatness!"

The couple is getting a bit agitated, and I use this to my advantage. "Greatness comes at a price, I'm afraid. If the limited number of points doesn't suffice, you can always consider an upgrade to our platinum package."

Thad's voice comes back gruff. "We already told you, it's out of our price range."

"Yes, I understand. However, you can take out a loan in your unborn child's name to pay for the upgrade."

"You want us to indebt our unborn child?"

"Forget unborn, the poor child has yet to be conceived!"

"Don't think of it as a loan," I say, another line from my script. "Think of it as an opportunity. With the advantages this will give the child in life, the loan should be easily paid in full by age thirty, and once paid off, the child will maintain all of the increased attributes."

"Should be?"

"Yes, there's still the randomness of the human experience, you understand. We only provide a genetic guarantee, but how those genes are expressed must be left to mother nature, as per international law. Not to worry, though, good genes invariably lead to good people. Our repayment rate is over 85 percent."

"And the other 15 percent?"

"Typically, that's from parents who don't spread the attributes wisely. We've since introduced stricter measures for our platinum package, and we expect that number to drop in the upcoming years."

Morgan leans in, drops her voice to a whisper. "I have one last question for you."

I laugh. Even if I hadn't eavesdropped on them in the waiting room, I'd be well aware of what she's going to ask. "Let me guess, sub-domains?"

The young couple's eyes light up.

"I'm afraid those violate international law."

"You really want us to believe that if some billionaire walked in, he couldn't pay to have his child's height altered?"

"If height were said billionaire's paramount goal, he could raise the attributes of domains he felt might affect height, such as attractiveness or athleticism. But there's no way to select for such specific human qualities."

"Why? I mean, I know it's the law, but nobody's ever been able to clearly explain why."

I know exactly why, but I play the part of the naïve office worker and echo the company line. "From what I understand, it's the same reason we can't offer a package above platinum. If humans were given the choice, they'd crank all attributes to one hundred. When everyone's at one hundred, nobody's at one hundred. We need these rules to maintain the human experience."

The young couple look at each other, whisper a few things into each other's ears. The amplification works well. They think I'm lying; of course, they do. I am. I hate when couples bring up the sub-domains, a topic I can discuss but not deliver upon. I need to redirect to the packages we do have, to the deals I can close. "The platinum package comes with an additional hundred points, allowing you to create a child that is well above average and poised for a successful life."

Thad won't admit it, but he's intrigued. "Remind me how much more the platinum package costs."

"Double the price of our gold package."

"Wait, double?" Morgan cuts in. "I read it was only a 50 percent increase."

"Yes, that's true, but that's for parents who are able to pay our price up front. Due to the risk of loaning to an unborn child, our fees do go up considerably."

The room falls silent as the young couple tries to process all the information being thrown at them. It's important for me to step out mid-meeting, to get an accurate sense of what the couple is really thinking, and now seems to be as good of a time as any. I get to my feet. "I can tell I've given you a lot to discuss. I'm going to run to the bathroom and give you a chance to think more about this decision. If you need anything, just open the door and holler."

I leave the room and peer through a strategically placed eyehole which gives me a full view of my office. My earpiece continues to relay what is being said.

Morgan turns to her husband. "What do you think about all this?"

He motions for her to be quiet. He reaches into a briefcase and produces a small handheld device resembling a ray gun. This is certainly an interesting development. He walks briskly throughout the room, aiming the gun at different surfaces. He sweeps the room with expert precision; it's clear he's been trained well.

"What on earth are you doing?" his wife asks. "What is that?"

"Quiet. Just give me a second." The gun emits a powerful ray that appears red to the human eye. He aims it at the walls, at my phone, at the underside of my desk, all the while saying, "Test." He's waiting for something to reflect back green. There's only one thing in that office that will come back green. I wonder if he'll find it.

His search comes back empty. He turns to his wife, speaking in a whisper. "It's illegal for them to record us. There's nothing to stop them from amplifying our voices, though. I wanted to make sure they aren't listening."

"Are they?"

"Not that I can tell."

"How do you know all this?"

"I just do." His voice is particularly insistent, and she lets the matter drop. "So what do you think?"

"It could be a good idea."

"I don't know, sounds like a scam to me. How would you feel if your parents took out a loan for you before you were even born?"

"How would you feel if your parents didn't give you every possible chance to thrive?"

"It just seems expensive, is all. What's the point of a great life if you spend the whole thing buried in debt?"

The questions are rather typical. I'm not really learning much that I didn't already know. The only real development is the presence of the ray gun. He's slid it back into his briefcase. I need to find a way for him to pull it out again. I press a button on my handheld device, which emits a staticky sound into the office. We use this when we want couples to feel they're being watched.

He takes the bait. He reaches for the gun and begins to sweep the room once more. He lifts my phone and scans the underside. I quickly reenter.

"I wish you'd put that down," I say, maintaining a professional voice.

He lets the phone slide from his fingers, tries to conceal

the item in his hand.

"We're not recording you if that's your fear," I say. "That would be highly illegal."

"No, it's not that..."

"We're not listening either."

He looks bashful. It's the first time all day I've seen an honest emotion out of him. The tough veneer has finally cracked; some humanity oozes out.

"I didn't think ordinary citizens were permitted the use of sound wave detectors," I say.

His eyes bulge. Another honest reaction. This time he's at a loss for words.

I reach for the form I had started to fill out earlier. "It says here that you work in construction."

"Well, yes, technically..."

"Technically?" his wife asks.

"Sound wave detectors are only permitted to those with government clearance," I say. "If we're going to process your loan, we need you to be honest with us."

"He's in construction," Morgan says. "Right, honey?"

Thad shifts in his seat. "Right." His voice lacks conviction.

"Mm-hmm," I say. "Except that's not exactly true, is it?"

Thad looks sheepishly at his wife, says nothing.

This is the chance I've been waiting for; one I rarely get. "Due to the inaccurate information provided in your loan documents, we won't be able to proceed with the gold package. However, as the loan for the platinum package would be in your child's name, we could still proceed. Please note, however, that this decision would have to be made today. Should you leave our office without a deal, I will have to file a report on your inaccurate loan documents that will invalidate you from further using our services."

"I don't understand," Morgan says.

"I think your husband does," I say. "I could step outside again if you'd like."

Thad says nothing but nods.

I reenter the waiting room with a newfound sense of interest. These meetings tend to go the same way; the presence of the sound wave detector has changed everything. I wonder if he buys my threat.

"They're listening to us, I'm sure of it," Thad says.

"How can you be so sure?"

"How can she know about sound wave detectors? She could only know if she had seen one herself."

"How can *she* know? How can *you* know?"

He stares down his wife, urges her to let the matter drop.

"If you don't trust them, we can go somewhere else," Morgan says.

"There's no point. Once they enter into the system that we used false loan documents, we'll be flagged everywhere. I think we better just go through with this. I can't be flagged. My boss will find out."

I can hardly believe my ears. He's doing my work for me.

"I'm just worried about the loan," Morgan says. "What if our child never pays it off?"

"We can account for that." Thad reaches to the monitor and begins to adjust the attribute bars, paying particular attention to measures like intelligence. The young couple argues back and forth. The confidence they had arrived with is long gone, replaced with a foreboding sense that any decision they make (or don't make) will doom their unborn offspring.

Morgan begins to fiddle around with her monitor, too, using the additional one hundred attribute points to build the perfect child who could fare well in the most important measures while retaining a sense of balance. Her apprehension begins to fade as she sees the ever-increasing scores.

Thad gets to his feet, opens the door, asks me to return. My eyes fall to the monitors in front of the couple. "Wow, both of your proposed children look rather similar!"

"They do, don't they?"

"It's the best of both worlds," I say, a line from my script. "The security of a healthy child, with the promise of an exceptional one. So, should we finish filling out that paperwork?"

It takes another fifteen minutes to fill out the form and explain the genetic testing and conception process that will take place. Thad stays uncharacteristically quiet. Morgan badgers me with questions that I am easily able to answer. When we're finished with the forms, I shake their hands and walk them to the door. "Remember, if you have any more questions, you should find all the answers on the pamphlet." I tap the pamphlet in Thad's breast pocket.

The young couple thanks me for my hard work and exits. They seem nervous but excited, as all new parents should be. I wait until they get into their car and drive off, and then I pull out my own sound wave detector and aim it around the room. "Test, test," I repeat. Most of the waiting room glows a faint shade of green, as expected, as the room has been built to amplify sound.

When I aim the sound wave detector at the stack of

pamphlets, they reflect a vibrant shade of green, a fitting color really, the color of money, the color of my money now that I've sold another platinum package.

* * *

This story first appeared in the After Dinner Conversation—February 2021 issue.

The Human Experience also previously appeared in Jared Cappel's short story collection of the same name.

Discussion Questions

1. Which, if any, of the things that take place in the story do you find the most immoral and/or disturbing and why?
2. If the technology was available to change the attributes of your child for a price, would you do it? If so, what attributes would you focus on and why?
3. Is it immoral to incur debt that continues on to the child if it goes unpaid by the parent? Does it matter that the debt is for a purchase that will potentially help the child's future?
4. If you could find out how you genetically rated on various attributes compared to the general population, would you want to know? If yes, what attributes would you want to know about and why?
5. What, if any, difference is there between a wealthy parent that is able to stay home, play with their child, and provide their child with mental stimulation so the child has the best chance at a good future versus the parents in the story who have the money to do this genetically? In both cases, aren't wealthy parents simply using their money to help secure their child's future?

* * *

Euthanasia

Kelly Piner

* * *

On a frigid December morning, Hank Sanders stomped the caked mud off his worn boots and entered Discount Hardware. He couldn't shake his cousin's remarks. *Put her down*, he'd said. The words had rolled so effortlessly off his lips, as if her life meant nothing at all, as if, simply by being old, she'd become too much trouble.

Hank marched up one aisle and down another, searching for a new blade for his knife. When had the shelves become so barren? It hadn't looked like this the last time he'd shopped there. But with the fuel shortages and the lack of truckers, was it any wonder? And where was everyone? He hadn't seen any other customer or any staff. With no one to help him find the blade or even care if he made a purchase, he returned to his old pickup, trash crunching under his boots.

He drove south, thirty miles along the Ohio River, where sheets of fog hovered over the water and worn concrete road. As he squinted and leaned into the wheel, he choked down his sense of loss for his nation. Once an abundant land of plenty, it now resembled a third-world nation with food and energy shortages. Little by little, residents were adjusting to lack and uncertainty. Incredible, he thought, how easily people could be conditioned to accept less and less.

At the fenced compound, he punched the access code into the keyboard, and a gate slid open, exposing a comforting wrought-iron sign that read: *House of Hope: Where Your Suffering Ends*. That sign had greeted him for as long as he could remember. In stark contrast, the massive gray government structure stood cold and uninviting just beyond the gate.

He drove to the back entrance and mentally prepared for another twelve-hour day. When he climbed from his truck, he avoided looking at the blurry mounds spread out on the grass. Through the darkness, he spotted a new shipment of crates that had been delivered during the night. It never ended.

Inside, he said, "Hi, girl," and bent over to pet the blue point Siamese that greeted him.

He'd often felt that Ling Ling had the gift of second sight, the way she seemed to sense the fear and dying spirits of those about to be put down and did her best to comfort them.

Hank flipped on the overhead fluorescent lights, and they made a hissing sound like that of a final breath being expelled. The sterile, concrete warehouse had no windows on the main floor. The only windows were in Hank's office on the second floor, facing the large cemetery out back. Some days, when he'd been outside digging holes for the smaller creatures, he could have sworn that he'd felt dead eyes staring at him. Just how many had he put down over the years? He refused to count. So many that the cemetery was full.

He checked his clipboard. Forty to dispose of today. He'd never gotten used to it, the death and misery he'd witnessed during his ten years running House of Hope, but he didn't want to think about that. Instead, he steeled himself and went about doing his morning inspection, going from one cell to another.

He donned a mask and entered the ice locker where the deceased rested, awaiting processing. It, too, was so full that now he arranged the overflow bodies on the ground by the cemetery. He checked his calendar. The eighteen-wheeler had last collected the corpses over two weeks ago. The crew had used a conveyor belt to move the dead bodies inside the trailer where they were stacked. What happened to them afterward, he didn't want to know.

In Euthanasia Cell Block No. 1, twenty dogs awaited euthanasia. However much he disinfected the cages between each use, they still smelled of death, and the animals all yelped for his help. He reached down and handfed a chicken-flavored treat to a toy poodle. Did the dogs understand that their owners had elected to put them down? And how many were really suffering, as opposed to having worn out their welcome through aging? No longer adorable puppies, many now required ongoing care as elderly pets.

And of course, the pet food shortage didn't help. Owners had grown tired of the weekly search all over town for dog food. Even here, the government refused to pay for pet food. The animals were being put down anyway, so why throw money away? But Hank refused to let the creatures suffer, so he purchased food out of his own pocket. He didn't mind the extra running around.

A chocolate Labrador, beautiful and bouncy, stuck his

paw outside his cage and cried. Hank opened the cage and petted the dog's head. "Who'd put you down?" he asked the distraught animal. He passed each cage and spoke kindly to every dog. It was the least he could do.

Put her down, played over in Hank's head like an endless tape loop. The knot in his chest tightened when he entered Cell Block No. 2, the feline room. He'd had a special fondness for cats ever since his mother had given him a marmalade kitten for his fourth birthday, and Hank had slept with Dylan every night of the cat's life. Now, a newly arrived marmalade, just like Dylan, whined when Hank approached, and he scratched the cat's neck. "It'll be okay, boy. I'd take you home if I could." He put the cat onto the floor, and Ling Ling rushed over and washed his ears.

In the beginning, Hank's dad had built a welcoming barn for the creatures they would take home. He'd even installed heat to keep them comfortable during the frigid Midwestern winters. But that had ended years ago with the government's No Removal Laws, forbidding euthanasia contractors from rescuing animals. Too many lives were unaccounted for, the government had said. Oversight was necessary for the welfare of the community. So now they kept strict inventory, and a hefty euthanasia tax paid for the centers.

His father had been the first operator hired by the government over twenty years ago. A soft-hearted man, his passion had been to humanely lay all forms of life to rest, however big or small. His dying wish had been that Hank would carry on the business.

Unlike his father, Hank didn't remember a time when the private medical sector handled these matters in their small practices. Still, when he had accompanied his dad to work, families hadn't simply dropped off a loved one to be euthanatized. They had delivered them kindly, with tearful goodbyes. But new laws had banished families from the compound. To make the whole process less personal, Hank figured, so families could more easily walk away.

He sometimes wished he could walk away too, but if he did, he'd have no way of knowing how the new operator would treat the "inventory." Most days, he wondered if he served any valuable function at all, beyond showing a bit of kindness to every poor soul brought to the facility.

Outside, he cranked up the forklift and moved first one crate and then another into the warehouse. When he'd moved the last one, he used a crowbar to open the first crate, smaller than the others. Inside lay a hodgepodge of tiny rabbits, guinea pigs, and lizards, all shivering from being left outside overnight. At least their owners hadn't just abandoned them on the side of the road, as millions of others were abandoned each year.

Hank rolled a heat lamp over to warm them. He saw no reason they shouldn't be kept comfortable during their final moments. He lifted a trembling bunny and wrapped her in a soft fleece blanket. In the past, he had occasionally broken the rules and had taken an animal home, despite the risk. If he'd gotten caught, he would have faced not only stiff fines but criminal charges, and he would have lost his license as operator of House of Hope. Since the enactment of the government's surveillance program, his every move was filmed, making it impossible to rescue defenseless creatures, so instead, he moved the menagerie into Cell Block No. 3.

As he had done for the past ten years, he prepared the supplies to euthanize the first group. As always, he avoided eye contact as he lifted a trembling dachshund from her cage and inserted the intravenous catheter into her leg. "I'm here with you, girl. It'll be okay," he said softly. Next, he injected a sedative to relax her. "Our Father who art in heaven," he recited before he inserted the death serum into her vein.

One by one, Hank moved down the line, avoiding eye contact as he inserted the death serum. He ended the procession with the Labrador, which he cradled in his arms as the dog gasped his last breath. Then, he moved the corpses outside onto the grass, where the cold temperatures would preserve their bodies until pickup later. He ran his gaze over the expansive grounds, where no fewer than five hundred creatures lay as if sleeping.

He hadn't known it would be this way when his dad had trained him as the next operator. The loneliness and isolation. But his father had pounded a strong work ethic into him, and Hank often worked seven days a week, carrying out his father's last wishes. He had never married. It wouldn't have been fair, being away from home so much. Ling Ling was his only constant companion during the endless days and nights when he elected to sleep on his cot.

"Ling Ling," he called, and the Siamese rushed up, meowing. "Come inside with Daddy." His hand trembled when he placed it on the knob of the main euthanasia room, Cell Block No. 4. He had unloaded four crates into the room earlier, and he took a deep breath before using the crowbar to remove the first lid under the watchful gaze of the blue electronic eye in the ceiling. It was always the same, the shock.

Inside lay an emaciated man, identified as Subject No. 36, age seventy-five. The old man's lips trembled as he struggled to speak. Hank leaned down, but no words of comfort would come. Did he have an incurable disease, or was the family just tired of caring for him? He'd never know, so he focused on inserting the catheter into the man's frail arm. He avoided looking into the elderly man's eyes, lest he be identified as the bad guy, the executioner.

It had once been an honorable institution, the euthanasia centers, after the new right-to-die laws were passed. No more lingering for months in cancer wards or in unsanitary nursing homes, barely remembering one's name. Finally, the sick could choose to end their suffering. In the beginning, patients and families met with a trusted physician, and together they made the best decision. But as with most well-intentioned programs, greed and corruption eventually got their fingers into the pot. Little by little, the dignities were chipped away until one day— he couldn't remember how it had happened—the trucks started delivering flimsy wooden containers. Supply chain shortages, the government had said. Crates, inhumane and barbaric, were plentiful and cheap, and no need to tie up limited emergency vehicles transporting those who would only be put down anyway. With too few resources and too many souls on the planet eating up limited supplies, especially the infirm and old, a single family member could elect to put someone down with only one federal physician required to sign off on the procedure. Now the sick and helpless were being shipped out like expired produce. How much worse it could get? He was afraid to guess.

Tears rolled down the old guy's face as Hank recited the Lord's Prayer for him. It was the least he could do to send the old man off with a little dignity.

In the next crate, a sixty-nine-year-old woman barely had a pulse. Her legs had already been amputated. Diabetes, Hank thought. He inserted the catheter and injected the death serum. He saw this as a blessing, ending her suffering. Maybe she had loved ones waiting for her on the other side. He could hope.

Hank removed the lid from the third crate. "Granny!" he shrieked.

Inside, his eighty-five-year-old grandmother, wrapped in only a flimsy white sheet, was identified as Subject No. 78. So much adrenaline shot through him, he could barely feel his body. *Put her down*, his cousin had said.

With bones as brittle as rotting wood, she looked as if she might turn to sawdust if he hugged her too hard. Her cheekbones and blue veins protruded through translucent skin. Gone was the luxuriant red hair she had always neatly arranged in a bun. Now, her nearly bald scalp showed through thin, gray hair. Still, her hazel eyes shone with kindness. Underneath the sheet, she wore only the pink flannel nightgown he had given her for her last birthday. Even in this state, she forced a smile, the crevices around her eyes as deep as tunnels.

His grandmother's face came in and out of focus, and a flood of emotions tore through him—disbelief, despair, guilt. He shut his eyes, praying it was all a bad dream. But when he opened them, he heard, "Dear God," as if a voice had come from outside himself.

Hank's mother had died of cancer when he'd been just five, and his dad had moved Grandma Kitty in to live with them. For him, she was more a mother than a grandmother. She had sugar cookies waiting for him when he returned from school, and she'd attended all his high school football games, sitting in the bleachers with a homemade afghan thrown over her legs. Hank had learned his love of animals from her as much as from his father. She had never turned away a stray and had volunteered her time at the local animal shelter where she'd taken Hank on weekends as a boy. "They give you unconditional love and exist on a higher spiritual plane," she'd said. Even as a child, Hank had understood what she meant. Now, as if sensing her love for animals, Ling Ling jumped inside the crate, purring and butting her head against Granny's cheek.

Could he have prevented this if he'd worked less and had spent more time with her?

He steadied himself against the crate and stroked her wiry hair. "Granny, who sent you here?" She'd gone to live with his Aunt Betty last year after she'd fallen and broken her hip. He could imagine Aunt Betty sending her away for extermination. She didn't even have time for her own children.

Granny gazed into his eyes and tried to speak. Just like the rabbit before her, she trembled from the cold as Hank tucked a soft blanket around her.

"I'm here to help you," he said, desperate to assuage his guilt and to make things right. He leaned down and kissed her cheek. But who was he kidding? He glanced up at the camera in the ceiling, ever watching. She knew what he did at the warehouse. He could see it in her eyes.

In all his years here, this was the first time he'd ever come face-to-face with a relative. He'd once put down a neighbor who'd been eaten up with cancer and then a teenager who'd lived on his street after the boy had been mangled beyond repair in a car crash. But this?

He closed his eyes and prayed for strength. So this was all

his granny's life was worth after she'd given so much of herself?

To hell with it, he thought. For a split second, he thought he'd rescue her. But then what? If he tried to save her, the authorities would catch up to them before he'd even make it home. He'd be taken away, jailed, and some stranger would unmercifully exterminate her.

She grasped his hand in her tiny, bony appendage and somehow conveyed her acceptance. It's all right, she seemed to be saying as she held his gaze. He steeled himself. The past ten years had prepared him for this moment. Even if no one believed it but himself, he served a valuable function. Treating every creature at the center with love and respect was his calling, his passion. Without a doubt, he provided the last glimmer of kindness any of them would ever know.

He leaned down closer, still looking directly into Granny's eyes. His voice cracked. "You're the best grandmother a boy could ever have had. I'm here to help you move into the light. I have to believe it will be peaceful and beautiful. Your suffering will end, and Grandpa will be waiting for you. Is there anything you want to say?"

Her lips barely moved, but her eyes conveyed the same love they always had.

Hank had the sensation of leaving his body as he quietly inserted the catheter into her arm. "Our Father who art in Heaven," he recited, and without guilt, he lifted the death serum and inserted it into her vein.

* * *

This story first appeared in the After Dinner Conversation—August 2023 issue.

Discussion Questions

1. What, if any, scarcity scenario would justify this kind of treatment for loved pets and the elderly? How bad would things have to get (*if ever*) for this to be okay?

2. What aspects of the euthanizing process are most offensive to you; being shipped in boxes, being barred from seeing loved ones in their final moments, being left in the cold, being left alone, being euthanized at all, or something else?

3. The story seems to imply the world situation deteriorated very rapidly, making the care of pets and elderly family members prohibitively expensive. Given the new global reality, what, if any, regulations would you put in place for having children or buying new pets in the future? Do people have an inalienable right to own a pet, have a child, and choose when they die?

4. The narrator justifies his role in this process by saying he, unlike others, treats those he is about to euthanize with dignity. Is this a better option than nonparticipation in an unjust system? Does the narrator believe the system is unjust or simply tragic?

5. What would you do if you were the narrator in this story?

* * *

In Defense of The Harvest

Rebecca L. Christophi

* * *

I know what you will all be thinking. It is true that I was asked to write this story by members of the current government. A government pertaining of a few politicians, lawmakers, and others who are currently subject to public scrutiny as possibly benefiting financially from The Harvest. The occurrences of the past few weeks have only heightened this concern. I find, however, that public scrutiny goes through phases. I have seen at least half a dozen of these in the past thirty-five years. Yet The Harvest remains.

I want you to know too that I was promised (and in-fact just finished reading through the contract before I began putting pen to paper, as the old saying goes) that not a word would be detracted from what I would write, whether it be in support or condemnation. As the first family to experience both tragedy and benefits from The Harvest, I am in a unique position to write on the topic. Indeed, I have spent most of my life since these events contemplating it and watching history unfold before my eyes, as we, as a country, changed the fabric of our society, and then of the world. I know I have been mostly silent on this topic but feel that now is the right time for me to speak out. I hope you will listen.

The idea for The Harvest was not new. As far as I know it was first put forth by a certain Dr. William D. Chomes, though I believe (based on my own research) that it was talked about in the medical community, especially among surgeons and physicians whose specific job was caring for the incarcerated, for many years before he wrote his polarizing paper on the topic. Dr. Chomes is now all but forgotten and it is, instead, Dr. Elizabeth Fortright, whose brother was a correctional officer murdered by an angry inmate with a blade hidden in his anal cavity, who brought public attention to Chomes' ideas.

Harvesting human organs from the dead to use in saving a life is a practice that had already been around for centuries and although there were still those who struggled with the idea (I remember my own grandfather telling me there was "no way in hell" he would let any damn doctor cut him up. If he ever ended up in a hospital, he'd be good and sure they had no reason to end his life earlier than God had intended), most people were reasonable enough to realize its extraordinary, almost miraculous, benefits. And the overwhelming number of stories of boys and girls being given a second chance at life were enough to shame any sceptics into silence.

My own Sadie was three when Dr. Fortright's ideas began to take shape in the public mind. There was a lot of buzz around what had happened to her brother, a lot of talk about her theories being based on revenge. But eventually, her own sincere and scientific way of writing and speaking began to win us all over. I say all, though of course, there were always those who disagreed. But as with most things, public opinion won in the end. And it only takes one clear voice to make something that a hundred years before would have been inconceivable, a reality.

Her arguments were flawless and concise. She found a lawyer to work with her, a policymaker, a correctional officer who had no affiliation with her brother (that way nothing would seem self-interested). I have met Dr. Fortright, and I can tell you, without reservation, that she is one of the most genuine people I know. Her goal was to save lives. Those worthy, or at least more worthy, of saving.

I hope you don't mind if I take a small breather here and tell you about my Sadie. Like most little girls are to their daddies, Sadie was the apple of my eye. She was the most innocent and mischievous thing you ever laid your eyes on. Her mother, Margot, and I were in our forties when Margot got pregnant. We had been told we couldn't have any more kids. Our only son, Rupert, was twenty-two. He had been a difficult child and grew into an unruly and ferocious man. Of course, we loved him. We were human. However, for our own mental health, we had long ago distanced ourselves from him. We had almost come to terms with the idea that our lives would just be lived between the two of us. Therefore, Sadie was the most incredible surprise. Margot's pregnancy, despite her age, was not difficult. Not as easy as it had been in her early twenties, but she did not complain. In fact, she often tenderly touched her round belly and spoke of how much she loved being pregnant.

So, Sadie arrived, and we both instantly knew, in the way only parents can, that this time would be different. She looked at us with such complete trust, such complete and perfect love. Her small dimpled cheeks, her round, soft fists, her smooth, tiny, pink nails. You have, truly, never seen a thing more perfect in all the world. And this never changed. Where Rupert had begun life pinching, kicking, crying, sucking on his mother's nipples until they bled, Sadie was gentle, her laughter like a song. Oh, she was still a kid, to be sure, with the silly mischievous ways of kids. She loved licking her fingers and sticking them in the sugar bowl, was always digging for things in her mother's garden and bringing the wriggly, many-legged creatures she found inside to keep as pets, often wanted more than we could give her, and sometimes cried about it. But, as much as a child can be, and I know you'll say I'm biased, but, truly, she was perfect.

Sadie was nine when Rupert moved back. She had never met him, and Margot and I rarely spoke of him. We had a few baby pictures in an album. Ones where he looked remarkably like Sadie, dimpled cheeks, soft brown curls and all. I never looked at these pictures. They hurt too much. Occasionally Margot and Sadie would. I suppose no matter what your children have done, they are still your children. We found out, much later, that Rupert's movements had been under observation by the FBI for several years. Of course, we didn't know that at the time, how could we? And though I have often wondered why they didn't do anything sooner; I find that particular thought trajectory leads down a rabbit hole I'd rather not go in. Besides, I have led a long and happy life and, at my age, I'd rather count my blessings.

Most of you already know some of the story, or at least think you know it. I believe it's now a regular part of high school history curricula. Rupert forced his way back into our lives the same way he forced his way into the world; tearing, screaming, fighting for all he was worth. It was a typical hot Midwestern June evening. The air was muggy and the mosquitoes were out in force. I was on the porch with a Miller Lite and Sadie was next to me on the swing reading some little novel, something about a spider, a Daddy-Long-Legs, I think.

Anyway, this black Oldsmobile skidded into the gravel driveway and out of it came a man I didn't recognize. He had thick black hair, almost to his shoulders, he was suntanned and muscled and wore tight-fitting dark jeans and a white tank. I kid you not, it was as cliché as that. I didn't recognize him even when he strode up the front steps in three long strides and grasped me by the shoulders, calling me "pops." It wasn't until I got a good look in his eyes, gray and flecked with yellow, like a cat, that awareness came to me.

"And who's this pretty little nugget?" he said, gesturing at Sadie. I didn't want to tell him, but didn't see any way of avoiding it either.

"Well, Rupert, that's your baby sister, Sadie. Sadie, say 'Hi' to your brother."

I think I must have been in shock because I don't remember much of the conversation. Mainly I remember Sadie. She was perfectly composed, perfectly polite, perfectly aware of everything that was happening.

"Hello," she said as she stood up and stretched out her small, freckled hand. Her voice was firm and clear, I remember that well, because my own was shaking. For a moment Rupert seemed taken aback by her directness. He paused, turned slightly, and I thought foolishly that he might go. But not Rupert, he was never one to give up. Certainly not when he had set his mind to something.

"Well, hello there yourself," he grabbed her hand and yanked her, hard, towards him, wrapping his huge arms around her, pressing her into him. I was horrified. It made me think of a lion caressing a mouse before he devours it, bones, hair and all.

At first he kept the anger at bay, trying to show us he had changed, but we knew it was just a matter of time. Like a kettle on a fire, at some point it's bound to start boiling. The first time he backhanded Margot across the face, I tried to force him to leave, but he was a very big man with hands the size and strength of two iron pans. I would have called the police, but Margot insisted I didn't. She always felt he was her fault. I wanted to disagree, to comfort her, but the mutation is, in a sarcastic twist of fate, inherited from the mother.

He did not try to hide his jealousy of Sadie. He would go into long rages and I remember his exact words, "You had the bitch just to spite me, to make sure I'd get nothing. You never did love me. But you damn sure do love her. The little whore." Margot would lock herself and Sadie in our room and turn the TV or the radio up to drown out the noise. I tried to stay calm, to let him rant, to try my best to understand him and have compassion for him. But mostly, and I'm no longer ashamed to admit it, I hated him. I couldn't stand listening to anyone let into Sadie like that, and I was working on a plan to get him to leave, in the gentlest way possible. I knew we just couldn't go on like this. I'm sure you're wondering about Sadie. She stayed composed through all of it.

We explained to her about her brother, about how he couldn't control himself and how ninety percent of men like him ended up in jail, and he was just trying to keep his demons at bay. We promised her we were going to do something about it soon. She assured us she was fine. It was during one of these conversations that the part of the story you probably know, happened.

He had just wound down from a rage, one where he threatened to kill Margot and I in our sleep and then do away with "the little bitch," sending us all to where we belonged, hell. He now sat exhausted in my blue armchair, and I thought he had fallen asleep. I went to the room with the girls, trying to comfort Sadie, who for the first time, seemed visibly upset. I was talking quietly, I thought, sharing with her my plan for Rupert's "relocation" as I was calling it, hoping to calm her.

It turned out, of course, that Rupert was not asleep. He was listening outside the door and when I was through explaining the details, came smashing through it with all the force of his six-foot-four, bulldozer body. I was just on the other side of the door but somehow my body was thrown in such a way that it only landed on my leg, crushing it just below the knee. I looked down and saw that where it disappeared under the door it lay perpendicular to the knee cap. In the same moment that I realized this, I also realized that Rupert had grabbed his mother by her hair and chucked her, quite literally, like a doll, across the bed, where she landed with a "thunk" on the floor between the bed and the dresser, her head smashing into the corner of the dresser just before she landed.

I know that after this everything happened quickly, too

quickly for either of us to act. I know this because it's what I've been told by forensic scientists, what I've had explained to me, and what, despite my own memory, I've come to accept as true. But in my mind, everything was excruciatingly slow. It was a motion picture run in reverse. Because I knew what Rupert was going to do. He had a knife in his hand, the prettiest little knife I'd ever seen. Silver and shiny, with a smooth black handle. It looked like a toy in his big hands, and part of me thought maybe that's all it was. Sadie began screaming before he reached her. But when he held her down and brought the knife close to her, staring down into her soft blue eyes, she stopped for a moment. I knew what she was thinking, she was thinking he wouldn't do it. Those eyes of hers had won her love her whole life, they wouldn't fail her now. But she didn't know Rupert. He cut them out one at a time while Margot and I watched. While we all three screamed.

It was sometime during the trial that Dr. Fortright approached us. She was kind, and tears glimmered at the corners of her eyes when she spoke of our Sadie. We knew she could be trusted; she had been through tragedy too. She was not pushy but laid out, laboriously, the details of law that she and a handful of others had been working on pushing through the legislature. She thought our case could be the clincher, the one to change everything. But, of course, it was up to us.

Margot and I talked about it long into the night, long into the foggy hours of the not-quite morning. For days we talked. We laid out each detail, went through them with a fine-tooth comb. Only the most hardened criminals, ones slated for death row or life in prison would be candidates. Each inmate would have a choice. Their parts could be harvested gradually, while they continued to live in the prison, or they could undergo a swift death, whereupon the various organs would be harvested after death.

The organs would only go to the most deserving, this meant, mainly, to children. The belief was that the practice, though perhaps shocking at first, would cut down on incarceration while at the same time saving the lives of many innocents. It would most certainly be embraced by the public, who already felt their taxes were being needlessly wasted on the overwrought prison system. Dr. Fortright and her team had only been waiting for the right moment. They had been waiting for us.

Margot and I talked, but really, we didn't need to. Each time we looked at our Sadie, we knew our answer.

It was a crisp day, mid-November. The leaves were sunset-orange and daisy-yellow outside our window. The doctors had made a makeshift hospital in our home. We had been adamant that there should be no press for this. The home-hospital was their solution. Dr. Fortright personally took on the guardianship of our privacy. Even making sure the surgeon, anesthesiologist and nurses wore plain clothes, only changing in the bedroom after they arrived. We weren't allowed in the room for the procedure so we sat, rocking restlessly on that same porch that Rupert took three long strides to reach just five months before.

Margot squeezed my hand and smiled at me when the surgeon came to get us. "You can see her now," he said. "She did beautifully, I think you will be very pleased."

He led us to the room, our room, that was now Sadie's hospital room. White and stark and smelling of alcohol. Margot and I each stood on one side of her and took a small hand as they slowly unwrapped the gauze, lifting her head a little where it was tucked underneath. "It's truly astonishing how far we've come with these sorts of surgeries in the last few decades," the surgeon said, smiling. "The recovery time is almost nothing. She'll be able to see you both almost immediately." Her eyelids, under the gauze were pale and ribbed with blue and red veins.

"We're here, darling," her mother said softly. "It's OK now, everything is OK, you can open them."

* * *

This story first appeared in the After Dinner Conversation—November 2021 issue.

Discussion Questions

1. Do you personally think organs should be harvested from the dead without their consent? Does the fact they are criminals change your answer about consent? Does their religious affiliation *(or lack of)* affect your answer?

2. The story says, criminals could have parts "...harvested gradually, while they continued to live in the prison, or they could undergo a swift death, whereupon the various organs would be harvested after death." Which parts of this plan do you agree or disagree with, and why?

3. Does a person on death row, or a person in prison for life without parole, deserve any rights at all? Can they be denied TV, internet, access to sunlight and fresh air, interactions with other inmates, or quality food? What rights should be guaranteed to criminals beyond the minimum to keep them alive?

4. What is the reason to keep a person in prison without the possibility of parole alive at all? *(Assuming the trial was fair, and it is more expensive to house criminals vs. put them to death.)*

5. Would you personally accept an organ donation from a criminal? What if they had not volunteered to give up the organ, but it was taken from them after they died? *(Before they died?) (If the process of taking it had killed them?)*

* * *

Two-Percenters

CJ Erick

* * *

Reginah stared at the crystal vial her friend Twylea had laid on her desk. A gentle light bloomed within the desk's frosty surface, illuminating the liquid sealed in the vial in shades of lavender.

"Go on," she prompted. Twylea could be annoyingly slow in disclosing useful context.

Reginah's friend, like all Socials, was divine-like in beauty, carved from alabaster and gold. Every pose, tiniest movement, or inflection in her voice was precisely tuned to thrill and disarm the observer. Even knowing this, Reginah often fell under her friend's spell. And today Twylea bore a gift.

"Imagine if you will," Twylea said, in the purr of a femme fatale, "a world where everyone could be a Two-Percenter."

Twylea was also intentionally vague, which she knew was frustrating for Rationals like Reginah. And she knew Reginah hated the commoners' label for her kind. It demeaned the Gifted's genetic superiority.

"That's been studied by hundreds of researchers," Reginah said. "The physiological and genetic inhibitions for those in the general population have never been successfully overcome. At least ten million commoners have died or been disfigured attempting it." She purposefully ignored the pretty ornament. "The council sponsors continue the research, but the consensus is it will never be done. Discussing it further is pointless fantasy."

Even for a "Two-Percenter," a genetically enhanced humanoid, Twylea was a stunning wonder, with enhancements focused on outward beauty, voice, posture, emotional expression. The perfect host, actor, debate panelist, politician. Inches taller than Reginah at nearly two full meters, body fit and toned with little or no work and built along Vitruvian mathematical proportions; flawless skin and golden hair framing her perfect heart-shaped face; eyes the color of the vial's lavender liquid, the color of wisdom, royalty, and first love; lips and cheeks and ears mathematically perfect; chameleon skin tone adapting to ambient light, mood, and purpose. Cleopatra or Helen or Aphrodite would pale in comparison.

Twylea's pianist's fingers tipped across the desk, and the inner light from the desk's surface sparkled from her golden nails. Her fingers stopped inches away and retreated. "Humor me for a minute." Reginah found she could do nothing else. "How many of us are there?"

"Here in the North American Region? Two per million. About one thousand. Worldwide—twenty thousand."

"How would you describe our influence?"

Reginah shook herself to clear her head. "Your Socratic

method is annoying. Get to the point." But Twylea just smiled. "Fine, I'll play."

Twylea's eyes twinkled. "Of course you will."

"Influence? We've been the driving force behind nearly every recent advancement—science, mathematics, physics, art... politics." She nodded toward Twylea as she spoke the last.

"For how long?"

"You know this, since 2045, when Orinheim and Hatomi perfected their recombinant techniques."

"And how far have we come in the last fifty years as a species?"

"Since the first hundred were identified and enhanced, trifold acceleration. Even our best statisticians struggle to define the rate of advancement. We continue to surpass the models."

Twylea smiled in approval, but it seemed bloodless, now that Reginah had withdrawn from her spell. Even her Social persona could not hide her inner tension from Reginah's Rational inspection.

"Yes. So imagine where we could go if all people could undergo the enhancements and not just the lucky few. Anything would be possible, perhaps even a final, complete understanding of the universe."

"Or total chaos, reminiscent of the Dark Ages. In the current structure, we lead progress, commerce, governance, albeit through shadow influence. There is no war, no poverty, little disease and that cured in weeks rather than years. The commoners recognize our superiority, if reminded gently on occasion, and we maintain order. But make us all relatively equal again—it could all break down. Or become obsolete. We just don't know."

Reginah cursed her friend silently, for wasting her time speculating worthless scenarios. It distracted from the work; twisted her mind in knots. "Either way, it would be 'Utopia,' in the Greek origins of the word—'No place.'—because it's never going to happen."

Twylea had let her disarming smile fall, something she seldom did. She bit her lip, something she never did.

"Do you think our privilege is fair?"

Reginah felt her friend's tension spread to her own thoughts. Why would Twylea push this question to her, a Rational? She wanted a Judicial, or a Sophist. Gratefully, she let Reginah off the hook and answered her own question.

"I don't," said Twylea. "For thousands of years, people have dreamed of gods coming from the sky to guide them, or feared others coming to make them pets."

"I know where you're going. We are not pet masters. Or puppeteers."

"We feed them. We keep water in their bowls, and even develop better ways to scoop their waste. And by not working to repair this imbalance, we sentence them to staying in their yards."

"At best, we are driving the new awakening. At worst, they live in pretty nice yards."

Twylea's smile didn't return, but her eyes turned their full mesmerizing power on Reginah. She pushed the vial inches forward with a finger so well shaped it resembled a ballet dancer's leg.

Reginah asked, "Is this a new deodorant for the yards?"

"You're very snide for a Rational. No, darling, this is the magic potion that turns all the pets into gods."

Twylea paused, expecting Reginah to provide the echo. "How?"

"Orinheim. He gave it to me before he... died." Dr. Benjamin Orinheim was the esteemed Rational presiding over the Bureau of Genetic Development, the agency through which all enhancements were orchestrated. Even among the Gifted, his name was spoken in hushed tones. *A god among gods*, she thought, then crushed it immediately. He'd died months earlier in a rare lab accident while repairing one of his gene-painting machines.

"Why did he spend his precious research time working on this problem?"

"Introspection. Regret, I think."

"Why did he give it to you?"

"He trusted me. I was selected to be one of his consorts."

"That bastard."

"No, I applied. This was Orinheim, Reginah. It made no sense for him to spend time pursuing relationships. But he still had personal needs."

"Maybe he should have 'enhanced' those away. And I'm not buying the regret explanation. He didn't create the rules that favor us. Why should he feel guilty to be Gifted?"

Twylea settled back into the formless ergo lounge, suddenly looking very human and very tired, like a five-a.m. harlot.

"I said regret, not guilt. He asked me to run an underground team to gather reports on the long-term effects of the growing class divide. Our findings were not encouraging."

"He carried on research without Institute sanction?"

Twylea's eyes twinkled again. "You would be surprised by

what influence can accomplish, even in Valhalla. What Orinheim wanted, he pursued."

It was Reginah's turn to sit back and feel tired. There was something very odd and yet suspiciously familiar about Twylea bringing the token and its story to her.

Twylea went on. "The edges are already starting to fray. The latest executive reports show more crime in nearly every district. Even violent crime, for the first time in 25 years, despite nearly universal surveillance and rapid response. Anti-government protests are growing in all seven continental regions. Psychosis, depression, suicide, all on the rise. And all of this supports our findings that things are not going well."

"And Dr. O's response was to make us all equal again, introducing a new age of unrestrained materialism, war, and class stratification beyond anything our best models can predict."

"Possibly. But no pets. No yards. No genetic lottery. No technological injustice."

"Just all the other really fine types of injustice. So why bring this to me? You have 'the cure.' Dr. O and his disciples believed this is the right thing to do. Why not release it to the world? Bring the New Age. Be heroes."

"His death wasn't an accident." Twylea's jaw was set, and her eyes drawn down, like Athena after she'd wet herself. "He couldn't live with himself not using it."

Reginah decided to wait her out this time, as long as it took. Meanwhile, part of her mind processed everything her friend had offered. The neural communications implant in her cortex accessed the Institute's Date and Records Library, and she reviewed the studies Twylea had referenced. Searching for an academic dagger, Reginah found none, no inconsistencies in Twylea's story. Of course, the foundation of her revelation, the secret studies and production of the contents of the vial, couldn't be corroborated, nor could she find any mention or rumor of them. So, none of it could be debunked.

Twylea sat forward again, eyeing the vial. "It adds a peptide sequence on three different chromosomes that simulate the family of genes that allow us to undergo enhancement therapy. Within weeks, most commoners can begin the enhancement treatments."

Reginah zoomed her eyes in, searching for telltales of molecular magic suspended in the liquid. But the genetic machinery, if it was there as Twylea said, was too elusory for even her enhanced vision. She shifted her spectrum further into the UV range, and the vial seemed to flare with neon fire. But it held its secrets, just colored liquid rocking in the faceted glass.

"So Dr. O solved the problem that a thousand studies couldn't."

"Yes." That, simply.

"The proof?"

"Thomas Belton."

"The late bloomer? I thought his parents raised him in a Regressive sect, and he was discovered late."

Belton had emerged in his mid-thirties, long after most Gifted were placed in the program. He had advanced quickly, now a Commercist, leading one of the three North American regional banks in Sacramento. Like most of the Gifted, Reginah had been identified at the age of seven during standardized testing, and her most suitable specialty gleaned over the next two years.

Twylea shook her head, a negative gesture that had crushed men's hearts.

"He was born a commoner. He applied for the research study, and Dr. Orinheim chose him for his age and demographic, and because his sect ties provided the perfect explanation. The transition took two years. There were others, many successful, but Dr. Belton the most so."

"So why hasn't this crossed over from the subjects to others?"

"The gene splicing is stable, and needs a vector." She nodded at the vial, but seemed to avoid touching it. "Dr. Orinheim chose a rhinovirus. The recipient develops a case of the sniffles, no more." She eyed the vial now with something like unhappiness. "And then they join us."

Reginah felt a safety valve about to pop, threatening to blow her annoyance all over the room.

"You're looking at that thing like it's a poisonous snake and not the healing elixir for all humanity's woes. There's a downside, obviously. Spill it, or stop wasting my time."

Twylea's frown deepened, and Reginah had to fight the urge to hug her. Her friend's voice dropped like a funeral recitation.

"It changes us also." And that, simply.

Reginah stifled a laugh. She'd at last deduced the real intention of this meeting. Twylea was conducting a psychology experiment, and Reginah was the subject.

"So I'm guessing we don't become double-gifted."

"No. At best, our enhancements are rejected over time, and we become... common, as you would say. Worse— debilitating handicaps. Worst—grotesque disfiguration and painful death." Her eyes swung up to meet Reginah's, and oh the act was excellent, award-worthy. A single tear gathered in Twylea's azure sea of an eye. "Socials suffer the most."

"How do you know this?"

"Dr. Orinheim modeled it, tried to eliminate the rejection. There were trials..." The tear she'd been nurturing slid down her cheek, like a fake glass pearl.

"Why me?" On the surface, her question meant why give Reginah the vial, but beneath that, why choose her for the study? Even as she thought this, a bristling pang of doubt pricked her mind. Damn Twylea and her agenda. Even Reginah's powers of logic and rationale couldn't protect her from the psychological hooks.

"Who else but a Rational, and who else among them but someone I can trust? Please don't hate me. I can't let it loose. I can't let it... I just can't. My niece, Freesia, a Social like me. I know it's the right thing—for the most people, for the future of our species—but I can't do this to MY people." She slumped, seemed to shrink into the body of a young girl, the person she had been before genetic magic had metamorphosed her into a goddess. "Please don't hate me."

As suddenly as a light going out, she rose and left the office. Left behind was the MacGuffin, the vial of colored liquid possessing incredible power. Or none.

After Twylea's after-image faded in Reginah's mind, she settled back in her chair, pushed herself down into a meditative state, and spoke the word that would trigger her mind into a deep trance.

"Spinneret."

Her mental processes divided into isolated silos. Her

persona, formerly called the "ego," stood aside much like a spectator at a sporting event, and she observed her logic center dissecting the inputs from Twylea's visit. She evaluated each of Twylea's assertions independently, categorized and filed them, and assigned multi-variable Monte Carlo probability curves to each. She then modeled a spectrum of systems, manipulating the individual assertions in hierarchical indices of weighted average relevance. Her communication portal again accessed the Institute's library to review relevant information in the databases. After these models processed the data to a resolution of initial findings, she adjusted those conclusions by analyzing Twylea's behavior, mood choices, and emotional expression. The algorithms churned for what seemed like hours, but when the processes were complete, she rose from the trance to find that only six minutes had passed.

With a certainty of 93.6 percent, she concluded that she had in fact been enrolled in a psychological experiment, with a similar certainty that her reaction and response would affect her future opportunities and career track. If it was a test, the vial contained only colored water, and the correct response was to smash it on a crowded walkway to simulate releasing the virus.

The most interesting aspect was that if Twylea's assertions were true and the vial contained genetic transformation, then the correct response was the same. The benefit of the many superseded the penalties for the few.

She needed a walk anyway.

She scooped the vial into her tunic pocket, took the tube down to ground level, then pushed through the building's security field and onto the softwalk. The crush of commoners on the walk spread away from her, giving her more than ample personal space as she melded into their flow, some nodding or tipping their sloped hats, most avoiding eye contact. The Institute discouraged special treatment for the Gifted, either deferential or negative, but their efforts were largely unsuccessful. The Gifted would never fit into common society any more than she could step onto this softwalk without causing ripples.

Likely under surveillance, she moved with the tortoise-like flow along the walk, stifling her inclination to press through them. The city was served by several modes of aerial and subterranean public transit, bullet tubes and sky buses, and many private options. And yet the press of walking humanity never lessened, as if there was an informal prohibition against modernity. The influence of fringe anti-progressive cults couldn't account for it.

Judging from the lack of fitness of the people near her and avoiding her attention, most of them weren't walking for exercise. Her nose informed that hygiene was also not a priority even in the summer heat. She could smell their disease and age and injury and addiction, in an effluvial miasma that identified all the ills that still pervaded the species. The best efforts of fifty years of Gifted influence had not ended these infirmities. Twylea's reporting that the vision of "perfect society" was regressing was borne out by the studies, both those performed by her people, and those of the commoner scientists.

These people were in decline, even as the work of Dr. O's group pushed the capabilities of the Gifted higher. Their problems had devolved into a race against time, the work to save these people. The seriousness of the stakes was exactly why this psychological study she'd been drafted into was so genius.

Eek, how piteous it would be to devolve from Gifted to commoner. Or even worse, to be crippled, a deviant, grotesque being, sub-common. She stifled a shudder, and wished for a strong breeze to freshen the city air. Almost on cue, the whoosh of a bank of urban ventilators kicked on, and a cool breeze carried with it the fragrances of clean linen and endorphins.

Ahead, two city blocks through the adaptive building towers, the city center park rested, like an Eden of green abundance. The circular softwalk around it was always filled with people, a perfect place to make her show of busting the vial and releasing the harpies.

Before she reached the park, at the next crossroad, commoners clotted the softwalk, gawking at some disturbance on the parallel roadway. She approached and the crowd parted, letting her pass. She didn't possess the arresting beauty of a Social, but she was still physically enhanced to a degree, and an impressive figure with clear dark skin and thick tresses of raven hair that she wore pulled back and tied. When she reached the curbed edge of the road, she found a vehicle accident, a cargo van stopped, and the burly unshaven man she assumed to be the driver. He knelt at the front of the vehicle, blubbering like someone insane.

"I didn't see her, I swear. She jumped out like a blur, faster'n the brakes could react!"

The "she" he referred to was Twylea, lying on her back on the pavement, partially under the van's front tracks.

The driver jerked when he saw Reginah. "I tried to stop, mum! I was too damn slow." He waved his hairy hands in the air above Twylea's face, afraid to touch her, or check for vital signs. From where Reginah stood, she could see none of the telltale signatures of life—chest rising, pulse in her neck and wrist, movement in her irises. Reginah didn't need to touch her to know the Social was dead. Reginah's throat clamped tight, so she could barely swallow.

To those pressing in around her, she asked, "Anyone call this in?"

An older woman about a foot shorter than Reginah, with limp graying hair and a pre-cancerous growth on her sallow face, said, "Yes, mum. I've signaled the Corp, and they're comin'."

"Very good."

The others crowded tighter, violating Reginah's space, risking the wrath of her discomfort. Some twitched the micro-cameras in their fingertips, capturing the scene. The driver buried his face in his hands. "Why did she do that? Oh god, I'm soooo sorry!"

Reginah willed the Social to end this ruse and rise, but she remained still and dead, with blood leaking from her sculpted ears and the corners of her temptress lips, the lavender pool eyes blood-rimmed and clouding over. Reginah forced herself to look away and surveyed the crowd instead, most standing motionless and stunned. Several men and women stared at Twylea and fondled themselves, apparently overcome by her beauty, even in death. Reginah felt her disgust rising like vomit. She wanted to strike them.

A few in the crowd were not staring at the dead Social. To a person, they were leering at Reginah with a combination of hatred and lust.

The wail of the Corp response team insinuated itself into her senses. To the older woman, she instructed, "Stay here until they clear the scene. Make sure you impress to them that it was not the driver's fault."

Which it wasn't. The modern auto-braking systems were nearly perfect at preventing accidents, and also vehicular suicide. Unless the victim was extremely motivated and quick.

She gripped the vial tightly in the bottom of her tunic pocket, and then stepped into the street and kicked Twylea's body once, hard, in the ribs. She ignored the squeals and gasps of the onlookers and walked away, leaving the smell of them behind her. At least the fool driver was shocked out of his inane sobbing.

She melded back into the flowing mass on the softwalk, back in the direction of her office, away from the city center, away from the crowds.

A few steps from her building, an opalescent tower shaped like a piece from an elaborate board game held the escalator down to the first level of the Under-City, a cavern of shops and restaurants that evolved almost nightly to address the changing needs of the populace. She paused and let the flow of commoners pass her by, all of them giving her a wide berth, but glancing back in curiosity. Rationals did not pause; they acted with decisive correctness, as if their actions would change the course of the future.

She pulled the vial from her pocket and eyed it, and her logic center fed her the new probability that it was what Twylea had claimed, well over eighty percent. There were dozens of commoners taking the escalator downward. She could toss it here and walk away.

Instead, she flicked the end of the vial off with her thumb, exposing the contents to the air. She raised it slowly to her nose and inhaled deeply, smelling ethanol, amines, potassium salts, and proteins.

She pushed into the flow of people, smelling their infirmities again. As she descended, she tapped drops of the liquid onto the handrail, then at the bottom wafted the nearly empty bottle back and forth among the throng. A young mother with a bluebell hair scarf pushed a child carriage with year-old twins dressed in the horrifying colors of pink and baby blue. When the mother looked away at a direction sign, Reginah sprinkled drops of liquid over the children's heads. She abandoned the empty bottle in a trash de-constructor.

She walked among the shops then, finding what she needed, a small auto-pay store that was serving as an apothecary by day. It would transform into a social club for dinner or recreational drug use in the evening. When she entered, faces turned toward her, like the dishes of radio receivers. There was one worker or proprietor, a man of perhaps 50 years, with a clear bronze face and ebony hair too nice, enhanced in the lesser ways available to a commoner with good finances. Surprised and uncomfortable, he watched her as she searched among the aisles, until she found the place where deodorants were displayed. Across the aisle, feminine cosmetics were arranged in colorful rainbow displays intended to hook the users. When she stopped there, examining the products, the man approached.

"G'day, ma'am. Is there something I may... assist you with?"

She gestured toward the cosmetic display. Her fingers were long and straight and sublimely shaped, and her nails perfectly symmetrical, without a cuticle. They would not remain that way.

"I'm," she said. "I'm... going to need... some of these things."

* * *

This story first appeared in the After Dinner Conversation—March 2022 issue.

Discussion Questions

1. Was it ethical to enhance 2% of the population in the first place, if the entire population was not able to be enhanced?

2. Does the human race have a collective obligation to continue to improve our species? Does the human race have any collective obligation at all?

3. It is okay for those with enhancements to have greater influence over the course of the world? Should the smartest make the policy decisions for the world? Is there a group that should have a greater world influence? Is there a group that currently does?

4. According to the reading, enhancing the 98% will wreck the 2%. Would anyone in the 2% ever volunteer to give up their place of distinction? If you were in the 2%, would you?

5. It is ever ethical to take away from one person, to raise up another? What about our progressive tax system that taxes the rich at a higher rate to benefit those with less? Can you think of other "real world" examples that you agree or disagree with?

* * *

The Decay

Sierra Simopoulos

* * *

The waiting room had the familiar smell of too much hand sanitizer. Benjamin studied the cover of a curled magazine promising "30 New Positions to Heat Up Your Sex Life" before letting his attention wander to the secretary who incessantly beat her pen against the counter while staring at her papers.

"Soltz, Benjamin!"

He started at the sound of his name. Gripping his cane, he made his way up to the glass box.

"Mr. Soltz?" the woman asked without glancing up from her papers.

"That's right."

"Says here you need to refill a prescription?"

Benjamin nodded, fumbling to get the pill bottle from his pocket before finally placing it on the counter.

"Some morphine and whiskey is what I really need, but I guess this will do." He smiled weakly.

The woman didn't smile. She continued to stare at her

papers.

"It says here that you've reached your allotted drug limit for the month."

Benjamin looked up, confused. "That's never been an issue before."

"The government just passed a new bill that it will only cover the first hundred dollars for citizens over sixty-five. Don't you watch the news? Anyways, you'll have to pay for it if you want me to refill this."

Benjamin reached for his wallet. "How much will it be?"

"Seventy-two dollars, ten cents."

"Oh." He slowly returned his wallet to his pocket. "I guess maybe I'll just buy some of that whiskey instead." He tried to smile, but only managed to pull his lips into a tight line.

The woman finally looked up. "Maybe take a look at some of your options, Mr. Soltz? For your sake and that of your loved ones." She gave a practiced smile and slid a pamphlet across the counter. "Zhu, Alice!"

Benjamin stuffed the pamphlet into his pocket and left the clinic. He walked down the mall concourse toward the subway with careful, shuffling steps. Around him, screens flashed from store windows. A screen showing an image of two women with perfect faces laughing together told him *Our NEW SPRING LINE is here.* A lingerie ad displayed two people pressed against each other, emblazoned with the words, *Live while you're young.* As he got nearer, the faint light of the facial scanner flashed in his eyes. The lingerie ad blinked and changed to an ad for Kingsford Whiskey.

* * *

Benjamin lowered himself onto his living room couch in

his small flat. His daughter Ania hated its ornate green and purple swirls, but he had picked it out with Felicity in their first year of marriage and he couldn't bring himself to throw it out.

He sat there for several minutes, watching the hand of the wall clock tick slow laps. He glanced at the TV remote, but the thought of cheery program hosts and never-ending advertisements felt overwhelming. Instead, he got up and made his way across the living room to the liquor cabinet. Moving aside empty bottles, he found one that had something left in it and poured the remainder into a glass on the end table. He lowered himself back onto the couch and took a sip. It was the kind of whiskey they sold at the convenience store, the kind that burned and smelled like burnt leather.

He looked at the picture of Ania that sat on the end table. She was grinning out from under a graduation cap. She looked happy here, happier than he had seen her in years. This had been the year before Felicity died. He remembered teaching Ania to climb the pear trees he and Felicity had planted in their backyard. He thought of the three of them hunting for worms together at Finn's Golf Course before their weekend fishing trips. A swelling pain rose in Benjamin's chest and his nose tickled unpleasantly. He chased the feeling away with another swig of whiskey.

His back began to throb from not taking his pain medication, and he reached instinctively into his jacket pocket for his pill bottle. Instead of the bottle, he found a crumpled piece of paper. He pulled it out, confused, and then remembered the pamphlet the woman at the clinic had given him. He smoothed it out.

Let us help you transition from this life well. The picture showed a young man and woman standing beside the bed of an elderly woman who looked like she was sleeping. The young people had big, perfect smiles.

He turned the pamphlet over. *You've lived an abundant life. Now it's time to pass the baton to the next generation. Our compassionate staff are here to make your last moments meaningful and comfortable. Medically-aided Cessation is a compassionate choice. Consider your options.*

Benjamin's hands shook as he stared at the pamphlet. Medically-aided Cessation. It was one of those topics that everyone thought about at some point when they were sitting alone and an ad for it popped up on TV, but of course it did not come up in polite conversation. Certainly, it was touched by conversation, "My aunt went to get put to rest this weekend" or "Toby's father is planning his going away party," but it was never talked about. Everyone knew people who had undergone the procedure. A few years before Benjamin had retired from Myers Construction, Francis, one of Benjamin's long-time coworkers, had not shown up for his Monday shift. It had been whispered, but never announced, that he had undergone the MAC procedure. He was a private man. He didn't like to make a big deal about these kinds of things. It was good that he should be at rest, after all. He had been a hardworking man, but now that his sight had been failing, what did he have left to live for? Continuing on would have been misery for him, the whispers had said.

Consider your options. His eyes lingered on these words.

At the bottom of the pamphlet, there was a phone number in large print. Benjamin glanced over to where his old telephone sat on the end table, covered in a layer of dust. He took another drink of whiskey.

Slowly, he reached for the receiver and dialed.

A cheerful woman's voice answered.

"Good afternoon. This is the National Institute of Life Care, Medically-Aided Cessation Branch. Could I get your name and citizen code?"

"Benjamin Soltz, 5N268FJ1."

"Are you calling to book an appointment?"

"I... well... I was just wondering... at what point in life do people usually make an appointment?"

"Well, it really varies from individual to individual. Most feel that when they can no longer live the life they want, it is the best option for them." There was a pause. "Are you considering the procedure?"

"I, uh..." Benjamin jammed the receiver back on its hook and stuffed the pamphlet into the coffee table drawer out of sight.

* * *

Ania had given Benjamin a new watch a few months ago. She had shown him how to scroll on it to do all sorts of things: listen to music, use the calculator, look at pictures. He didn't remember how to do any of that now. He just wanted to make a phone call. Ania had said that she had saved her new phone number on the watch somewhere. He flipped through all the screens, squinting at the little glowing symbols, but didn't see anything that looked like a phone number. He scrolled through all the screens again and even tried clicking on one of the symbols, but it just opened another complex screen with some sort of graph on it. He exhaled heavily and got up from his kitchen table, piling his plate from breakfast on the others beside the sink.

He sank onto the couch and flipped the TV on. He didn't really watch, but it was good to be surrounded by the sound of other people's voices. Suddenly, his old telephone rang. *Ania.* He snapped off the TV and sent the remote skidding across the coffee table as he scrambled to grab the receiver.

"Hello?"

"Hello, is this Mr. Soltz?" Disappointment flooded Benjamin. It was a woman, but not Ania.

"Yes," he said. "Who's this?"

"Mr. Soltz, I'm calling from the National Institute of Life Care. We saw that you inquired about the MAC procedure, and I just wanted to see if you had any further questions about it."

Benjamin felt a pang of panic.

"N-no. No questions."

There was a brief pause. "Well, we are always here if you do."

"Well, j-just one question, actually..." Benjamin thought of Ania and felt his eyes grow wet. "Do people who get the procedure usually still have family?"

"Yes, quite often they do," the woman said. "Many feel that when they can no longer contribute to society or to their family this is the best option for them."

"What makes most people feel that they can no longer contribute?"

"Oh—well—there are different factors for different people. Being unable to contribute financially or posing difficulties of care on their loved ones. It's something everyone has to weigh for themselves."

"How do family members usually respond?"

"Well, many people decide not to tell their family members to prevent them from having to feel the guilt of agreeing with the decision. But others have family members who are supportive."

"I see. Thank you. G-goodbye."

"You have a good day, Mr. Soltz. Feel free to call if you have any further questions." There was a sharp click.

Benjamin stared at the receiver in his hand for a long time.

* * *

The doctor said that Benjamin's morning walks were an important part of his overall health and wellness. Benjamin's lower back throbbed with every step and he leaned heavily on his cane. He'd gone through the bottle of subsidized painkillers before the end of the month again, even though he'd tried to spread out the dosage more than usual. As he made his way laboriously down the sidewalk, he was startled by a buzzing from his watch. He pressed repeatedly on the glowing screen.

"Ania? Ania?"

"Dad?" His daughter's voice sounded distorted.

"Dad, you're muting it. Stop pressing the screen. You only have to press it once. Listen, I'm going to stop by your place in twenty minutes."

"Sure, sweetheart." There was an electronic bloop and the call disconnected. "Ania? Damn thing!"

It had been months since he had seen her. His mood lifted and even his backache seemed to lessen.

He stopped at one of the fruit stands, where a lady he often bought from was resting under an umbrella. Ania had always loved pears.

"How are you, Helen?"

"Oh, you know, getting by. My little tyke just learned how to crawl. He's been making a real mess of the house."

"Oh? How old is he now?"

"Ten months. The little menace. He managed to pull all my baking supplies off the bottom shelf of the pantry yesterday. Spilled the cocoa powder everywhere!"

Benjamin cracked a small smile, peering over his thick spectacles at the fruit prices. He raised his eyebrows.

"Why are these so darned expensive?" he said, nodding to a tray of golden yellow pears.

"Ben, don't you give me a hard time." She shook a finger at him. "They're organic. And rare to find, mind you. Almost all the fruit these days comes from the vertical farms. But there are always those rich blighters who are asking for the organic stuff. It was a real pain to find a farmer willing to ship here."

"Are they any better?"

"Oh yeah. They're delicious—sweet and juicy to the core. I'd eat them all the time if it wouldn't break the bank."

"I'll take one. Do you mind wrapping it up for me? I don't want it to bruise. It's for my daughter."

Helen obliged, and Benjamin smiled as he tucked the pear in its brown-paper wrapping carefully into his jacket pocket.

* * *

Benjamin moved around his flat as quickly as his rheumatism would allow, putting dishes in the sink and throwing a blanket over the couch to cover its old pattern. He opened the window, hoping the fresh air would make the place more appealing and hide the smell of stale whiskey. His watch suddenly vibrated again.

"Dad, I'm here."

He tried to press the watch face to respond when there was a knock on the door.

"Come on in," he called as his daughter pushed the door open.

"Why did you buy me this thing?" he asked, pressing on the watch in irritation.

Ania laughed. "You never used the phone I bought you. Besides, this is what everyone has now." She was wearing a small black dress that her mother would never have approved of and was carrying two bags of groceries.

"Well, come on in. Have a seat." She smiled as he gave her a one-armed hug around the groceries before seating himself on the couch. "How's the new job? Do you like being an immigration—whatcha call it?"

"An immigration case analyst. It's been really good."

"You know, I helped build the Kay Building just a block over from where you work. Can you see it from your office?"

"No, I'm on the west side."

"Oh. I was the project manager on that job, you know."

"Yeah," she gave a small smile, "you've mentioned it. Dad, I can't stay long, but I was in the area and I thought I should come by and make sure you were taking care of yourself and bring you some food." She set the bags of groceries on his kitchen floor and began unloading them into the fridge. Chicken, lettuce, tomatoes, a bag of pears. The pear in his pocket suddenly felt like a foolish gift. She had a good government job, while he was living off the pittance his pension gave him. She could buy herself organic pears whenever she wanted.

"I thought you were going to stay and talk awhile."

"Oh, Dad, you know I'd want to if I could. But some of my old university friends are in town, and I'm going to take them out."

"Oh, I was wondering why you were wearing that." He waved at her dress.

"Well, I can't let these good looks you and mom gave me go to waste." She flipped her long hair over her shoulder and flashed him a joking smile.

Her watch began to ring. "Dammit! Lane is calling. I gotta run, Dad." She kissed him on the cheek and headed for the door as she answered the ringing machine. "Lane, I'm so sorry! I'll be there in a few minutes. Just meet me in the parking—" Her voice was cut off as the door closed behind her.

A jolt of pain went through Benjamin at the sharp sound of the door clicking shut. He leaned against the back of the couch. For some reason, his heart was beating fast. There was a tight feeling in his chest, but his eyes were dry.

Abruptly, he got up and headed for the liquor cabinet. He shoved bottles to the side, digging right to the back corners, but all of them were empty. He cursed, knocking over bottles as he withdrew his shaking hands.

His mind flicked to the coffee table drawer. He'd kept the thought of its contents forcibly out of his mind, but it lingered constantly at the edge of his subconscious.

He slowly opened the drawer and pulled out the pamphlet. He read it again. Then, he dialed the big number.

"National Institute of Life Care, Medically-Aided Cessation Branch." It was a man's voice this time. "What is your name and citizen code?" Benjamin gave them.

"Our records show that you've called about an

appointment before?"

"I... yes. Yes, a little while ago. I was just wondering... about the procedure... how does it work?"

"Well, once you book a date, we'll have you come in to the clinic here. We'll go over any important last wishes and legal matters, so you'll want to make sure you bring any necessary documentation. We take care of all that with our in-clinic lawyers to make sure everything is as simple as possible for the client. Our staff will be here with you the whole time to make your last moments meaningful and comfortable. The procedure itself is straightforward and entirely painless." He paused. "Did you have any other questions about it?"

Benjamin didn't respond. A few months ago, he had decided to surprise Ania at her home. He had picked through all the flowers in the grocery store to find the best ones and even splurged on some wine with a fancy French label. Finding her place had been difficult. That side of the city had changed so much over the years and he had started to become nervous that the faded piece of paper with her address referred to a building that wasn't there anymore. But finally, he had found it, feeling rather pleased with himself. A man had opened the door, squinting and rubbing his eyes.

"What'd ya want, man?" His breath smelled of liquor.

"I was just stopping by to visit my daughter." Benjamin straightened up. The other man blinked at him stupidly.

"Ania? She's out."

"When will she be back?"

"She's a busy woman. Probably not until late tonight," said the man. Benjamin's shoulders slumped.

"Would you give her these for me?" He held out the

flowers and wine.

"Sure, man, sure." The man took them and closed the door. Benjamin had hoped Ania would call him when she got home and saw that he'd been there. But even though he stayed awake later than usual, he didn't hear from her.

"We have an availability this afternoon you could come in for."

"Oh... I... I was thinking maybe a few weeks from now?"

"It is of course your choice, but we highly recommend the procedure as soon as possible after the decision is made—it helps avoid any unnecessary stress or pain. Let me know what you prefer."

There was a long pause.

"Are you still there, Mr. Soltz?"

Benjamin remembered Ania at six or seven, smiling down at him proudly from where she had climbed up on the roof by scaling one of the trees in the backyard. Felicity had been nearly hysterical, but Benjamin had laughed, calling her his little squirrel. She had been so pleased with herself until she tried to climb back down. Suddenly, she burst into tears, kicking her legs as she held onto the roof and struggled for purchase with her feet. Benjamin had been up the tree in an instant, catching her legs and drawing her to the trunk.

Tears began to roll down his cheeks. He thought of her as she had been this afternoon, rushing out to meet people he had never heard of. She had moved on from the back garden to a world of glass office buildings, a world where she didn't need him.

"Mr. Soltz? I can book you in for six o'clock if you'd like."

"Six o'clock would be fine."

* * *

Benjamin had to take the subway all the way downtown to get to the clinic. Every time the subway stopped he gripped his cane shakily with both hands. A woman got up from her seat a short way down the car. Benjamin shuffled carefully in that direction. A teen blaring music through his headphones slid into the seat.

* * *

The glass doors moved smoothly to the side as Benjamin entered the clinic. A bright-eyed woman who stood just inside directed him to the palm scanner. The blue light under his hand flashed and the woman checked her tablet.

"Ah yes. I see you have an appointment for 6:00, Mr. Soltz?" Benjamin nodded. "Right this way, please."

She led him to a room with a large, four-poster bed, a small wooden desk, and a manicured tree in the corner.

"If you will just wait here, Doctors Emerson and Schneider will be with you shortly. Feel free to make yourself comfortable."

Benjamin sat on the edge of the bed. It smelled vaguely of lavender.

The door opened and a man and woman entered.

"Mr. Soltz? Pleased to meet you," said the man, smiling and extending his hand. It was warm and firm. "I'm Dr. Emerson and this is my colleague, Dr. Schneider." A woman with very red fingernails took his hand. "We are here to discuss your transition from this life," continued the man. "First of all, do you have any questions for us?"

"Um. I—I want to tell my daughter. But I don't know how."

"Mr. Soltz," said the woman, "sometimes the best thing we can do for someone we love is to free them from the weight of having to choose. Many people's family members feel the obligation to try to dissuade someone from making this choice, even if they know it's best. We recommend, though this is of course your choice, that you make this decision on your own so that your daughter doesn't have to carry the weight of worrying that she made the wrong decision after you're gone."

Ania would try to stop him. Benjamin knew it. His heart lightened at the thought. But it quickly plummeted again. She'd put him in some expensive home, and he'd be even more of a burden on her.

"Many patients write a letter," the woman suggested, "for after they are gone."

Benjamin nodded.

"Yes, I'd like that."

The woman took out a stack of thick paper and a pen. "We know this can be an emotional time, so we'll leave you alone to have some time to write. Just press the button on the wall when you are finished." She set the materials on the desk, and the two doctors left the room.

Benjamin picked up the pen and started to write in his slow, careful hand.

* * *

Dear Ania,

He paused, trying to process what he could say.

I'm sorry I didn't tell you about this decision before it happened. I didn't want it to weigh on you. I know you would have taken care of me, but I didn't want to be a burden to you. I don't want you to feel bad now. I want you to live your life to the fullest. I'm going to have them leave you everything. It's not much, but with the money from the flat hopefully you can buy your own place and be more secure than your mother and I were when we started out. I love you so much and I'm so proud of you.

All my love,
Dad

* * *

He read it again and his eyes teared up in frustration. It felt flat and inadequate. It didn't say all the things he felt at all. But he didn't know how to say it any better. He set it down on the desk before pushing the button on the wall.

The male doctor re-emerged almost instantly with another man who he introduced as the in-clinic lawyer.

The legal proceedings were quite quick. Benjamin told him everything was to go to Ania and signed the places he needed to. Benjamin was then left alone again for a few minutes and moved back to the bed, shifting around as he sat on the edge. Finally, the male and female doctor came back.

"Everything seems to be in order," said the man. "Now, we also want to thank you for considering the future of our nation with this decision, Mr. Soltz. It's important that all citizens think about how their lives fit into the rest of society. With limited funding for medical care, this decision could allow a young child to have the resources to have the lifesaving operation that they need. You are a hero, Mr. Soltz. As a gesture of our gratitude for your decision, the government will cover all the expenses for this procedure and the funeral and will also plant a tree in your name."

"Would you like to choose your tree, Mr. Soltz?" asked the woman, holding out a brochure.

Benjamin looked up. "Maybe a pear tree?"

The woman's smile faltered for a split second. "I'm sorry, Mr. Soltz. That isn't one of the options that we have on hand. How about we plant a nice poplar for you?" She pointed at the glossy picture with one of her red nails.

"Oh... That would be alright."

"Mr. Soltz, I'm going to ask you to lie back here on the bed and relax," said the man, pressing gently on Benjamin's shoulder. The bed was overwhelmingly soft. The duvet was going to swallow him. Panic began to rise. He would never see Ania again.

"You are doing the right thing." The woman looked down at him with that perfect smile. "This will help you relax." She covered his nose and mouth with a mask. His vision blurred.

He had to see Ania again. He had to hug her one last time.

He felt a sharp prick in his arm. A moment of terror filled him. It died away quickly.

* * *

The mortician unzipped the bag to remove personal effects and clothing from the body before cremation. He placed the wallet and keys in a demarcated container. While removing the man's jacket, he noticed a strange lump in the coat pocket and pulled out a bruised pear wrapped in brown paper. He dropped it into the trash bin.

* * *

This story first appeared in the After Dinner Conversation—April 2022 issue.

Discussion Questions

1. The woman on the phone tells Benjamin that people choose to die when "they can no longer live the life they want" or because they are a burden to their family, or unable to contribute financially. Do you think any of these are good enough reasons to choose to die?

2. What, if any, is a good enough reason to choose to die? Do people have a moral obligation to stay alive as long as possible?

3. Should Benjamin have told his daughter what he was going to do before he died, or did he make the right decision in sparing her the guilt of trying to talk her out of stopping him?

4. If you were able to talk to Benjamin, what would you have advised him to do?

5. What is the societal purpose for someone like Benjamin? Are people required to have a valuable societal purpose to justify their use of limited resources?

* * *

Visions of Midwives

C.S. Griffel

* * *

The heavy groan sounded as though it were being dragged from inside the woman's body involuntarily. Her pregnant belly heaved as guttural sounds enveloped the tiny bedroom. Keery dabbed the sweat from the woman's forehead. The midwife, Luanne, examined the woman to check her dilation. A clock on the mantelpiece ticked away the minutes, piling them into hours.

"Illona, you're doing so well, darling. Your baby's head has engaged, and you're going to really start pushing."

Illona responded with only a nod and "uh-huh."

"Keery, come here, girl," Luanne ordered. Keery obeyed quickly. "Place your hand here. Feel that? That's how you can tell the baby's head is engaged. Illona, on your next contraction, you're going to push." Keery was nearing the end of her apprenticeship, so it was not the first time she had felt a baby's head engaged. Still, she obeyed. Each experience was building Keery up, readying her for her practice.

The process went quickly. It was Illona's sixth baby. Within a few pushes, the baby's head was completely born.

"One more big push, Illona, and your baby will be born." Illona's contraction hit; she scrunched her face until it looked like a closed fist and pushed. Luanne's hands grabbed ahold of the baby as he was suspended in the space between being born and not yet born. The elderly midwife's eyes rolled back as a vision of the child's destiny encompassed her mind. The moment was over as quickly as it had come. The little boy was born. For the briefest moment, Keery saw that Luanne's features were grim. Before Illona could see her face, she wiped it clean of emotion.

"Is it a boy?" Illona asked, her voice breathy and rough from the effort of getting her child out into the world.

"Yes, it's a boy," was Luanne's dry reply.

Keery looked at the tiny baby. He looked perfect. He balled his little hands into fists and kicked with both his legs. She wondered what Luanne had seen. Keery had not yet experienced the second sight, but she knew she would when her turn came to be the attending midwife.

"Take care of Illona, Keery, while I take care of the mite."

Keery's job now was to wait for Illona's body to complete the process of birth. Soon the placenta would appear. Illona did not know that Luanne had seen her son's future. It was a secret long kept by the midwives of their people. The clock tower in the town square chimed out a quarter past one in the morning. Keery noted that the little boy had not yet cried. Illona noticed too.

"Is he all right?" Illona's voice, roughened from groaning, broke the quiet. Luanne did not respond immediately.

"Midwife, is he all right, I say?" At this, Luanne wrapped the boy in the soft blanket his mother had carefully knitted for him. Illona didn't have much in the way of wealth, but each of her babies at least got a new blanket, even if it was knitted from yarn carefully undone from his dad and grandad's old sweaters.

Luanne brought the little man to his mother, only his face visible in the mass of soft yarn, just yellow enough to not be white. The midwife handed the waiting mother her child. The mother's eyes were full of fear and love. She glanced at her baby's face, his closed eyes.

"He never drew the first breath of life," Luanne delivered the words gently, but they struck the mother like a fist to her gut. The woman gathered her baby to her, and a wail like the cold winter wind barreling through the high mountains grew out of the woman's belly and shattered the peaceful calm of deep night.

Keery wondered what had happened. She had seen the boy born. He had been kicking and balling up his tiny fists. She knew he had been alive. Confused, Keery glanced at the senior midwife. Luanne's face was a mask of stoic resolve. It was not the time or place to ask questions.

Upon hearing her mournful wail, Illona's husband rushed into the room. He climbed into the bed with his distraught wife and drew her and the baby to himself. He murmured into her ear that he loved her, would always love her, but he did not tell her to be quiet or that it would be okay. He simply allowed her to pour out her grief. Uncaring that they had an audience, the husband held his distraught wife, lest the pain take her away with her child.

Keery helped Luanne gather their things quickly. It was

best at this point to leave the grieving family to their pain. It would be the father's job to care for the wee body now. Before they left, the father said, "Your payment is on the mantel, good wife." It was ill luck, even under the circumstances, to leave the midwife unpaid.

As they walked through the damp cold of the night, Keery struggled to put her question into words. What had happened to the child? She alone knew that the midwife had lied. That baby was alive when it was born.

"Luanne..." Keery began. Luanne anticipated the question.

"Child, you will understand when you birth your first baby. You will know when you see what the future has in store. That child was destined for great misery. 'Twas a mercy I done. It is a burden we midwives carry, the purpose of our gift." Her words were sharp and final. Keery knew she would answer no more questions. They parted company near the town square, Luanne to her snug, well-appointed home, Keery to the hovel where she still lived with her parents.

Keery did not sleep that night. She kept thinking of the tiny, perfect arms and legs, unused to the immense space outside the womb, making small, jerking movements, feeling for the boundaries of its new life.

The waning summer brought with it many births. The cold nights of December—all the harvest work done and winter settling in—brought with it many conceptions. Husbands, no longer exhausted from the hard labor of spring, summer, and fall, more frequently sought the affections of their wives.

August was the midwives' busiest month. It also brought an end to Keery's apprenticeship. "There are too many babies coming for me to hold yer hand any longer," Luanna told her as

July closed. "We'll place you with the younger mothers who've already had a babe or two." These tended to be the easiest births. The mothers were young enough that the risk of complication was low but had already proven their ability to birth healthy babies.

Keery was summoned for her first birth on August 5th at one in the morning. It was, of course, a full moon. Luanne's errand girl, Peony, rapped loudly on the door, waking Keery and her parents. Keery would not be able to move into her own home until she had earned enough from attending births to purchase one. Her vocation as midwife meant that she would never have a husband. She did not mourn this fact. She had seen many women, married in the rush of youth's lusts, walk an unhappy path when passions cooled. She had also seen young couples wed soberly and advisedly and remain in love their whole lives. Her chances, she supposed, were as good as any to go either way. She simply knew that it was not her destiny to wed. It was part of the midwife's second sight.

"Mildred Connor has gone into labor and needs attendance," Peony said urgently. "Mistress Luanne is attending Morgrid's birth and cannot leave. It's not going well. She sent me to fetch you. She says you must attend Mildred on your own."

Keery nodded and grabbed her midwifery satchel. It had been a gift from the Midwives' Guild and still smelled and creaked like brand-new leather. "Tell Mistress Luanne I'm on my way." Peony scurried quickly into the darkness.

The walk to the Connor's home was about twenty minutes. Mildred's husband answered the door with a look of relief on his face. "It's going quickly," he said. Keery nodded in response and followed him to the back room where Mildred lay upon the bed, knees tucked back as far as they would go, sweat dripping gently down her forehead. As Keery walked in, Mildred was gripped with a contraction that made her push with all her might. Before Keery could reach her, Mildred's body reflexively pushed out a baby girl. Keery moved to check the baby was all right while Mildred took deep breaths, an automatic response to normalize her breathing. When Keery's hands touched the baby, she received no second sight. This child's destiny remained in the realm of the unknown and the unknowable. It happened often enough that a baby was born before a midwife could arrive, especially with healthy babies. It is only in the moment when the child is suspended between being born and not yet born, when the head has emerged, that midwives receive the sight. Frankly, Keery was relieved. The burden of knowing another person's destiny was frightening, and she was glad to put it off, if even for one more day.

Keery checked over the baby, who showed every sign of being quite healthy. After cleaning the baby, Keery handed her over to her mother, who cooed over her beautiful child in the way just birthed mothers do. "Hello, my darling," she purred into the child's ear, "aren't you pretty?" Mildred rained kisses upon the head of fine, raven black hair. Keery waited with Mildred until her placenta was born, checking that all was well. When mother, child, and happy family were well settled, she slipped into the bright midday sun, pleased with herself.

Coins jingled merrily in Keery's little purse as she strode through the village on her way home. It wasn't until Peony crossed her path that she noted the somber air of the village. "Peony," she called, "how is Morgrid? Did her child fare well?"

Morgrid and her husband had been childless for the first twenty-three years of their marriage. The couple had long since given up hope of ever having a child when Morgrid found she was finally pregnant at forty-two.

The child looked up at Keery, shaking her head, "No," she said. "Morgrid and her babe died."

It was common for there to be complications in birth for first-time mothers in their thirties or forties. Keery was saddened but not shocked at the outcome. This, too, was a part of midwifery, dealing with the loss of mothers in birth. The midwives did all they could to shepherd mother and baby safely through the process, but sometimes, there was nothing they could do. Death was fated.

It was three weeks later when Keery was summoned once again to attend the birth of a young, fourth-time mother. When Keery arrived, the woman's husband answered the door, drunk. "She's in there," the man said as he pointed to a room on the west side of the house, his stance unsteady. Three young children huddled together in a corner. The eldest sister, no more than eight, sat in between two little boys, looking to be about five and three years old, respectively. The sister's arms were protectively draped over the shoulders of her little brothers. She had a hardened look in her eye, something sad to see in one so young. The little girl made eye contact with Keery, and a little smile crossed the child's lips, a welcome for the young midwife. A groan came from the westward room, and the child's eyes darted back to her father as he shouted, "Quit yer yowlin! It's giving me a headache!" Hardness replaced the brief smile in the child's eyes.

"Why don't you step outside, sir, where your wife's cries

won't bother you. She'll be fine now that I'm here. It looks like your girl there can look well after her brothers." The man nodded, stumbled out the door, and headed for the pub, Keery was sure. He looked like he had once been handsome, but drink and misery had twisted him into an ugly facsimile of his younger self.

The woman in the bed clung to the headboard rails like a drowning person might cling to driftwood in a raging river. Unlike her husband, prettiness still lingered on this woman's face. Love for her children kept her from total despair.

"You're Agnes, aren't you?" Keery inquired. The woman nodded in reply. "I'm Keery, the midwife. I want you to take some deep breaths." Agnes obeyed and breathed in deeply through her nose. Predictably, Agnes's labor went quickly. She seemed to relax with her husband gone and a midwife present.

No more than thirty minutes after Keery's arrival, the baby's head emerged from the birth canal. Keery placed her hands on the tiny head to support the child as its mother completed the birthing process. When the vision overtook her, the pain was so intense Keery thought she would explode into dust, down to the very last molecule. The sensation lasted only a moment, but within it, Keery felt what seemed an eternity pass. She knew now what Luanne had told her about. She knew this child would experience intense suffering. Yet, as she looked at the tiny, beautiful little girl, now fully born, she knew she could not do what Luanne had done. Keery didn't know if this meant she was cowardly or courageous. She only knew she could not extinguish the light of life burning in the milky blue eyes now blinking up at her.

Keery handed the child to her mother. "A lovely little

girl," she said. And like all mothers, Agnes drew the child to herself, murmuring and cooing.

"Margery," Keery heard Agnes whisper. Whatever else may come in this child's life, she was loved and content in this moment with this mother.

Misery did come to the child. When Margery was just three years old, Agnes came to a sad end. A merchant in the marketplace allowed his eyes to linger upon her too long. Her husband, in a drunken and jealous rage, beat her to death, and he was hung the next morning, leaving their four children orphans. No one could afford to take in four children, and they were all separated. Within a few months, the families that had taken in the children woke to find their beds empty. The eldest sister had come in the night for her siblings, unwilling to be apart. What became of them after that, no one in the village knew. Keery surmised the child had gone to the city and taken up prostitution to keep her siblings under a roof and fed. There was appetite enough in the big city, even for very young girls, to keep body and soul together for the little orphans. Keery wondered if she was wrong not to have released Margery from this fate.

Most of Keery's visions portended a mixture of pain, sorrow, joy, and peace. All human lives have some of everything. Of course, there were lives that held more or less joy, more or less pain than others, but she had not yet again felt the pain that had been foretold for Margery. Keery, carefully saving every coin, now lived in a small cottage of her own. It was not ostentatious. In fact, it was small and lacked any luxury, but it was tidy and her own. Keery was now a well-loved midwife, popular with young mothers.

Keery awoke naturally in her own bed for the first time in three days. She had just overseen a first-time mother, and the labor had been slow. Even so, baby was well born, and mother was resting in the glow of new motherhood and the love of a proud husband. She looked at the clock on her mantelpiece. It read 10:00 a.m. Keery felt positively indulgent. She made herself a trencher of cheese and bread and poured a large glass of ale. Tucking in, she enjoyed a leisurely meal by the fire. No knock at the door disturbed her while she swept and dusted her little cottage. She even made it to evening mass. It wasn't until four the next morning that a knock disturbed her rest. Birgitta Hoskin was in labor. She and her husband, Tobias, lived in the manse, the largest home in town. Tobias was a merchant. Keery was lucky to have been chosen to be Birgitta's midwife. The fussy young mother required a lot of attention, which meant Keery was called to the manse for frequent visits. Each visit added more coins to her meager stash. Keery was not greedy by any means, yet she dreamed of delicate curtains adorning her little kitchen window, softening the glow of streaming sunlight.

Birgitta was buxom and well-built for childbearing. Though it was her first baby, her labor was rapid. Her body just seemed to know exactly what to do. It was ready to send baby number one into the world and prepare itself for birthing the next nine that would surely come. Birgitta's baby was crowning within an hour. When her hands touched the blood-stained head of the child, Keery felt something she had never felt before. The terror of a thousand souls ran through her in one split second. Another push from Birgitta and the child was born, and Keery's vision gone. The child would not suffer, she knew, but would cause great suffering. It was a boy lying limply in her hands with the umbilical cord wrapped around his neck. Keery's throat tightened. What should she do? The child had not yet drawn breath. She could let him expire. She could save many from suffering, were her vision to be trusted. It would be easy to say he had been born dead. He had the cord wrapped around his neck. Birgitta was anxiously peering at the midwife and baby through her spread knees.

"Is he all right?" Birgitta asked. Keery looked up at the question and saw in the mother's eyes fear and love for her baby. She looked back down at the limp body, bluish around the lips. He was a perfect baby otherwise. Sweet, like all newborn babies. Without further thought, Keery loosened the cord and coaxed breath into the baby's lungs. Soon, he let out a mighty wail. Keery handed him over to his waiting mother. Stoically, Keery finished the rest of her duties, waiting for the placenta, cleaning and clearing things away, and packing her bag. She left a happy mother with a nursing child as she slipped out of the manse.

Once again, Keery was plagued by the fear that she had done the wrong thing by letting a child live. When she arrived home, she did not unpack her things for her customary cleaning. Instead, she knelt before the little altar in her living room. The statue of the Virgin Mother, wearing robes of robin's egg blue and a gilt crown, had been her one indulgence. It had made a deep gouge in her savings. She prayed to it now, her heart pouring out her fears before the saintly young mother depicted in wood. Was she wrong to allow such suffering into the world if she could stop it? Was Luanne right? Was the purpose of the gift of sight for snuffing out suffering? She looked up at the statue, its beatific eyes staring perpetually up to the heavens. She would get no answer here. Keery looked at her hands. They had helped usher many lives into the world already. She wouldn't use them to usher it out. Perhaps she would answer for it one day. She prayed the virginal lady would speak up for her when the time came. A knock at the door caught her attention. She sighed and stood. It was Peony.

"Astrid's water broke," the young woman told her.

"Tell her I'll be right there."

* * *

This story first appeared in the After Dinner Conversation—April 2023 issue.

Discussion Questions

1. Would you be willing to work as a midwife if it meant seeing the future of the child being born?
2. Should any baby be put to death under any foreseeable future? Is there any situation where killing the newborn is the right choice?
3. In the story, Keery hesitates in her decision to allow the birth of a child who will live to cause misery for others. More so than when she decided to allow a child to be born into experiencing a lifetime of misery. Do you agree with this distinction?
4. Would it be better to tell the parents of the child's future so they could choose whether the child lives or dies? What are the pros and cons of this approach?
5. What, if anything, is a practical distinction between killing a child in the story and terminating a pregnancy in modern society when a severe genetic defect is found?

* * *

On Good Authority

Peri Dwyer Worrell

* * *

Eufala, Alabama 02/19/2053

"Dr. Totter, may I speak with you about the security measures for your trip?" Zane, bearded, muscular, was poised and looming over her, and she fought the urge to take a step backwards.

Vivian Totter looked over her shoulder at the lookout tower's viewing window. "So, you tracked me down!" She turned from the view of the no-man's land between the concertina-wire fences to face him. She'd always loved taking a bird's-eye view this way. "I was just taking a few minutes' alone time. So much has happened since the vaccine tested out."

"Yes, ma'am," Zane drawled courteously. He shook her soft doctor's hand with his hard warrior's one. "It's a great thing you did. Wiping out the zombie virus for good!" He grinned, quirked smile blooming through his blonde beard like a wild spring crocus, appealing in such a seeming brute of a man.

Vivian's chest swelled with pride, restrained in favor of

humility. There were still so many possible slip-ups! But if they could get enough people vaccinated to build herd immunity, there would come a day, in her lifetime, when no one would ever have to watch a loved one turn into a flesh-eating zombie again.

"We've got a long way to go before that happens," Vivian said. "As the transmission chain's broken, there'll still be a lot of infected subjects to hunt down." She tilted her chin at the wall of hirsute human muscle standing before her. "There'll be work for people like you for a long time to come."

Zane preened ever so slightly under her glance and she found herself swallowing hard. His searching awareness demanded she lock gazes with his blue eyes.

He blinked, moment over, smiled deferentially. "Have you traveled in the armored units before?"

"Short distances."

Zane briefed her in his tranquil drawl: "They're not too comfortable, for sure. But they *are* safe. As for the threats we'll be facing: It's important that we all stay alert. Even though, with the vaccine, almost no new ones are converting, they still live three years." He tensed and added, "—As I'm sure you know!"

"That's right. Three years, more or less." She nodded.

He relaxed back into his authority. "And everyone within about sixty miles of here has been vaccinated, so there've been no new infections. It's a beautiful thing, Dr. Totter," he said. "They're fading away, slowly but surely." His voice jittered with barely contained excitement. "But, as we get outside that sixty-mile radius we'll start running into deaders again...thick. We'll be four cars," he continued, "first and last car, armed security, the second you and your grandmother. Umm, Doctor Totter, are you sure you want her to come with? It's not gonna be easy. The roads are damn rough and we may have to go a while between food and, er, bathroom breaks. There could be some engagements with zombies. It could be really unpleasant." .

Vivian chuckled. "I won't tell her she can't go, and I'm willing to bet you don't want to, either! Grandma's pretty spry for 75. We'll cushion her seat real well, and she's already rigged up a diaper for herself. She eats like a bird. As for 'unpleasant,' Grandma got me and my ma out of Huntsville and into this compound safely when the shit hit the fan back in '23. I'm willing to bet she could tell some stories might scare even you!"

He put his hands up in surrender. "Okay, okay, just making sure. Anyway, it'll take about four hours to reach our first waypoint."

Zane opened the door and stood back to let her descend the watchtower steps. She didn't look to see if he was watching her body from behind—too disappointing if he wasn't. Ever since the vaccine had passed its quick-and-dirty clinical trial (n = everyone in Eufala), people had begun to defer to her authority, and she wasn't used to it. She was barely used to being in charge of the medical team at the compound since Ralph retired: two other doctors, six nurses, and herself. The only one of the lot who'd been to actual medical school was Ralph, now approaching 80; he'd trained both her and her colleague Dillon. That was the norm nowadays; the population centers that supported big universities and teaching hospitals just didn't exist any longer. Which made it even more critical that Viv's new vaccine could be synthesized easily in a minimal micro lab, which most of the enclaves had.

The two of them emerged together from the darkness of

the tower, blinking in the sunlight. "Jed and Cindy," he nodded at an athletic young couple nearby, "will be riding with you. Jeff and me, we'll be in the third car with the mayor's aide and her wife. Samuel and Dan will be taking point and Tom and Tyler will bring up the rear." He pointed out four well-armed, sturdy, young men loitering about near the watchtower.

"Sounds good. I'm packing a small bag," she chopped one foot by two in the air in front of her, "and so is Grandma. Will that be a problem?"

"No. In fact, we have room for more if you need to bring it. You should see what that aide is bringing!" He rolled his eyes and winked. They both laughed.

That night, Vivian dreamed about Zane's azure eyes.

* * *

The next morning, Vivian and Grandma were standing in the central square of the compound in the pre-dawn twilight. Grandma pulled her sweater snug in the cool morning air of northern-Alabama winter. Vivian caught her profile and was startled anew at her hunched posture, fragile hands, thin hair (once black, now fully white), and the way the sweater hung deflated on her. There was no denying that the hardships since the Outbreak had taken their toll on Grandma Emma. For a moment, she wondered if the trip was a good idea, if it might be too hard on her. But then Emma Totter turned her brown eyes in Vivian's direction, and the flash in them reminded Vivian that her fire, though banked, still burned bright.

"Let's get this show on the road!" Grandma demanded impatiently.

"Soon, Grandma," soothed Vivian. "Getting a group of sixteen people all going the same way at once is like herding cats."

The sun had just cleared the horizon when they finally climbed into their vehicle and settled in. Cindy was at the wheel. Vivian had seen her about the compound but never knew her by name. Her hair poofed under a bandanna and her open smile contrasted with the taut, ready muscle of her brown arms. She wore a revolver as a sidearm and had her rifle slung over the back of her seat.

Zane leaned into the rear of the vehicle and handed Grandma and Vivian each a shotgun. Vivian took hers, checked the load, "Buckshot." She set it diagonally across her lap pointed up and out; Grandma did the same. Zane nodded approval and moved on to arming and checking the rest of the convoy. Jed settled in, riding shotgun with one shotgun, a full-auto rifle, and two semiautomatic pistols with extended magazines. The four cars all checked in on the radio.

Jed said, "Our average speed on these roads is about twenty-five miles an hour. Cullman's expecting us, and we'll radio them so they can let us through their gates. We stop overnight there."

"Cullman? That's where Grandma's from!" She smiled at the old woman, who nodded. Her hearing was excellent for a woman her age, and one who'd been exposed to more than a little gunfire, at that.

"Hmm. It's also the only enclave between here and Huntsville." The taciturn Jed spoke tersely into the radio, "Let's do it!" And the convoy rolled.

But first, the compound's crew went through the gate-opening protocol: two people on foot into no-man's-land, inner gates closed. Rattle gates, fire two shots, wait five minutes. One zombie came out of the woods and lurched towards them. Garcia stage 4, Vivian automatically assessed: hairless, monocular, integument and underlying fascia macerated, sex indeterminate, missing appendage (foot). The two crewmen waited patiently for it to lurch to the fence. A patrol stepped up and leveled his shotgun. The blast sprayed the creature's blackened tissue into the air, morbid confetti that rattled as it hit the ground. No other zombies showed, so they opened the inner gates, the convoy drove into the no-man's-land, forming up between the fences. They closed the inner gates and opened the outer ones.

"Only one deader. That's phenomenal!" crowed Zane over the radio. "A year ago there would have been at least eight or ten. *At least!*"

Cindy spared a moment from scanning their surroundings to glance back at Vivian. "That's down to you, Dr. Totter. You're gonna save the world!"

Vivian waved the praise away. "If it hadn't been me it would have been someone else."

"But it wasn't someone else, was it?" said Cindy, "it was you! Eufala's very own. And we get to drive you to Huntsville to get an award!"

Cindy had to concentrate on driving. Zane had said the roads were rough, but that was an understatement. The past three decades, anyone who'd ventured outside the fences for highway maintenance took his life in his hands. They'd done the bare minimum and sometimes not even that, so the roads had deteriorated—asphalt slowly crumbled, then gravel washed away. In some places the roads were no more than dirt tracks; in other places the dirt-track detours were more passable than the gullied roadbed. The summer was wet, so they had to watch for mire that could trap the trucks. Cindy eventually stopped apologizing to Grandma, enthroned on her feather pillows, for every bump.

Once the convoy reached the rise overlooking Cullman, they examined the survivors' compound. It had once been a monastery of nuns, but the grounds were now surrounded by a buffer of concentric chain-link and concertina-wire fences, just like home. Inside the fence was a jumble of huts, motor homes, tents, shanties and lean-tos, lining the barrier and extending all the way up to the monastery's august rock cathedrals, halls, and dormitories.

The vaccine hadn't yet begun to transform life in this community, and they had a precious crate of vials earmarked for Cullman. As they approached the settlement in the hollow, there was an especially bad stretch of road, where they were forced to slow to a crawl to avoid breaking an axle or ending up in a ditch. The cars slowly rocked and bumped their way along, Emma jostled and shaken, uncomplaining but plainly uncomfortable. The truck chassis clunked and the transmissions groaned. Predictably, zombies emerged from the underbrush, drawn by the noise. Thorny vines clawed shreds of skin from them as readily as clothing as they lumbered out, indifferent to the losses. Several blocked the lead vehicle, and two clawed at Vivian's side window.

Vivian gazed at them dispassionately: one was freshly metamorphosed, she assessed, within the past 48-72 hours. Judging by skin tone and resiliency, Garcia 1. It slapped its palms to the window, showing intact distal extremities. It clawed ineffectually with fingernails that still bore traces of polish. It also had still relatively undamaged hair and clothing. In dim light, it could have passed for a human, a ponytailed blonde. The other was skeletal, its lips and eyelids desiccated and fallen away to reveal a staring rictus, its hair a patchy, matted broom. It swung its ropy, fractured arms like slings to strike the window. It was missing all but two fingers on one hand and missing the other hand from the forearm down. Garcia 3+/4-.

"Defensive action," hissed Zane over the radio.

"Copy that," Jed responded, unlocking his passenger door by hand, jumping out, and landing in a semi-squat, swinging his shotgun to bear. Cindy thumbed the door lock closed before Zane hit the ground. Jeff, Zane, and Dan (or was it Samuel?) were outside their vehicles. Tom and Tyler, in the unmolested back car, didn't even bother. Vivian and Emma clutched their shotguns, but the fighters outside seemed bored, all in a day's work, as they blew the infected away like kids plinking bottles in the woods.

The caravan rolled into Cullman right on schedule. Just like home: decayed zombie bones hung from the concertina wire and littered the ground outside. A few, freshly snagged, twitched or writhed on the razor-sharp spines.

As the convoy approached the gate, they stopped about 100 yards back and radioed their presence. Four security men once again jumped out, one from each vehicle, holding rifles this time. A squad of fighters from the enclave, toting shotguns, piled out of the inner gate, which closed behind them. The convoy's fighters dropped back, and the compound's guards fired a series of blasts in an overlapping fan pattern to both sides, well clear of the convoy. These shots took out a few zombies at close range, but there was one, Garcia 1, a teenager with intact skin, cornrows, and barely soiled clothing, that caught only the edge of the spray of shot and kept coming towards the convoy; Zane took aim with his rifle and made an easy head shot.

The outer gates swung open and the convoy crept through, rifle shooters backing up at the rear, staying at ready until the outer gates closed. Only then did the inner gates swing open.

Vivian emerged from the vehicle, stretching and swinging her arms before turning to help Grandma out. As they straightened, an elderly nun in antiquated floor-length black habit and white wimple stepped up.

"Dr. Totter?" she said. "I'm Sister Elaine. Welcome back to Sacred Heart." Her blue eyes peered out of furrowed cheeks at Vivian's face, seeking recognition.

"Welcome *back*?" asked Vivian.

Sister Elaine flinched as though someone had elbowed her. "Oh, of course you don't remember! You were just a child! It was your mother..." Sister Elaine caught sight of something urgent she had to do in the next room and abruptly scurried through the door, calling behind her, "Sister Veronica will be with you in a moment."

Sister Veronica, young and painfully effervescent, stepped up almost at once and introduced herself first to Grandma, then to Vivian. Grandma set out on her own before the introduction was finished, as if she already knew this Benedictine abbey.

Sister Veronica trotted to overtake her and steered Grandma and Vivian to their austere guest-of-honor quarters, a bedroom with two single beds with patchwork quilts, two wooden desks with wooden chairs, and a small chifforobe.

"Please join us for dinner in the dining hall. Turn right here, up one floor, across the corridor, and downstairs past the library. The bell rings at 6 and dinner is at 6:15." Vivian looked at her vintage self-winding watch: 3:05. She spent the next half hour getting Grandma and herself settled in. Grandma wanted to nap, but Vivian felt hungry and restless, so she went out to explore the grounds. Maybe she'd run into Zane.

A roughly circular walk divided the refugee city and the monastery. A gazebo was centrally located among the ramshackle dwellings, low zigzag crowd-control fences leading up to it. A table and supplies suggested that it was used as a daily soup kitchen. The families she saw were diverse and mingled freely, but loose districts of Blacks, Hispanics, and whites formed a crazy quilt of permanent encampments.

As she wandered around the big circle and passed a man with a white beard and mustache pushing a wheelbarrow of tree limbs and yard trash. He stopped, perhaps ten feet away, and said, "Carrie!" His tone and expression were broadly cheerful, as if addressing a pet or small child. Then he shook his head, muttering, "No! Can't be. Are you Carrie's daughter?"

"Yes, that's me! Vivian."

Before she could step forward to shake hands, he shook his head and growled, "Should have slit her throat. Saved us all the trouble." Vivian faltered, speechless, bewildered. He shuffled his wheelbarrow past.

She had no luck bumping into Zane, so she made her way to the monastery dining hall per Sister Veronica's instructions. The plain room, large and low-ceilinged, held eight-foot communal tables and folding chairs. At the end of the room, she saw the bustle of people fixing to serve the evening meal via the kitchen pass-through. She helped Grandma into a chair and wandered over to offer help with dinner.

She waited at the counter, watching the women inside run mixers, ladle grits, scrape griddles, and lift huge steaming trays out of industrial-sized ovens. A sixtyish woman approached, rolling a cart of plates and cutlery. The woman startled.

"Oh! Oh, it's you. I mean, you look just like your mother. Oh, dear, I... I'm so sorry." The woman blushed, then scurried away. *Hmm.* No one seemed to need help, so Vivian took her place across from Grandma.

Grandma looked at Vivian over her book. She peered closely at her face. Grandma sighed and set the book down. "What have they said to you?" she asked. So, there was something going on. Grandma would come clean. The old lady was forthright as a shovel to the back of the head and mean as a rattlesnake when she needed to be.

"*Said?* Nothing! But that's the third person who's mentioned my mother and then spooked and run away."

Grandma patted her own chin with a wilted hand. "I should have told you sooner. What do you remember about your mother?"

"Not much," Vivian answered slowly. "I know she died when I was almost four. I remember sitting on her lap, her rocking me. Holding me and rocking and humming." Vivian closed her eyes. She treasured that one memory of her mother, would reach for it when sleep eluded her, could hum the simple melody, one bar over and over, until her breath evened out and she drifted into an ocean of moonlight and soft currents of breeze. Just thinking of it now, the anxiety of this conversation seemed a little less urgent.

"Do you know how she died?"

"From what everyone said, I assumed a zombie got her. Young as she was, that's how most people go."

"That's right, child. That's right." Grandma hesitated. A long time. Her brown eyes seemed fixed on something far away. Vivian leaned forward, and that made up Grandma's mind to speak.

"Vivian, your mother was not right."

"What do you mean, 'not right?'" Asked Vivian.

"I mean, simple. What we used to call retarded. Later they called it mentally challenged. Developmentally disabled. Whatever you want to call it.

"I was only nineteen and in college when she was born. I had no idea I was pregnant, almost until the very end. I drank like a politician. I wore loose sweatpants and baggy shirts in the dorm and showered when no one else was awake. When I went into labor, I told myself I'd eaten something spoilt.

"There was so much blood! I finally called 911—" Vivian tipped her head questioningly.

"That's the number we used to call when—oh, never mind!—I called for help. It took them four hours to find me on campus. By that time, your mother Carrie was in deep trouble."

"I see," said Vivian, and she did. She knew what anoxia from hemorrhage could do to an infant during delivery. Vivian didn't remember her mother ever walking with her, talking to her, and suddenly it all made sense. "My mother was brain damaged at delivery. But, how did she die then?"

"Just as you thought: A deader got her. She was 13. She was scheduled for a hisstersalpothingy..."

"Hysterosalpingectomy?" suggested Vivian. "Exactly."

"You were going to *sterilize* her?"

"It was what was done. There were too many people, not like now, my dear. It was all perfectly legal. We had a court order and I'd signed off as her guardian. But then the zombies started coming and things got bad. I got us out of Birmingham and came here."

A few early arrivals had drifted into the dining hall. The bell rang: 6:00. The cutlery and dishes were set on the counter in the window and platters and trays of steaming food were set out, but Vivian's hunger had vanished. She spotted Zane sitting down at a table with the rest of the security crew, but that hunger seemed to have receded as well.

"So," she asked, "who was my dad?"

"We don't know for sure," said Grandma. "But we think it was a boy who looked after her in the afternoons when I was at work. You look exactly like her—exactly. *Except* her hair was curly and yours is straight. Like his. He knew she was getting the operation. We think he took advantage." Her wizened lips pressed themselves.

Vivian recoiled in disgust, then moments later was absolutely gobsmacked by the knowledge that, without that rape, she wouldn't exist. She looked at Grandma, who was studying her from under hooded lids. Grandma knew what was going on in Vivian's mind. At the very moment Vivian worked it out, Grandma continued.

"You were born here. You spent the first four years of your life here at Sacred Heart. Sister Elaine was your first babysitter. I had been an oblate here..."

"Oblate?"

"Kind of a try-out status to becoming a nun. It was years

earlier. I decided it wasn't for me and left for college instead. But the nuns treated me as one of their own all the same, when we came with the other the refugees. We lived here in the dormitory, you, me and Carrie, and about forty other women.

"The fences weren't double back then. A big storm came, washed out a gully, and a zombie managed to squirm through the gully and right up to the chair where your mother was sitting in the sun. Before anyone knew it, it had taken a big bite out of her."

Vivian closed her eyes, dazed, queasy.

"Emma!" exclaimed Sister Elaine, coming up at that moment with her food tray and sitting next to Grandma. "Let's catch up! But first let's get you something to eat. You must try the cornbread. It's Sister Gertrude's specialty."

She took Grandma's arm and the two older women headed for the line at the window. Vivian's appetite had sagged, but now it surged, a full-body hunger that had nothing to do with pleasure, and she followed, served herself. She ate reflexively, hardly tasting, speaking in monosyllables. Grandma excused her to the others as fatigued, both from her journey and from working around-the-clock on the vaccine.

Vivian went to bed early, and dreamed of an infected subject squatting on the ground and giving birth to another infected subject who immediately squatted down and gave birth to another, ad infinitum.

* * *

She woke with her teeth fitted together like the jaws of a trap, her tongue imprinted on the insides of her molars and jammed against the roof of her mouth. She sat up into a headache at the base of her skull. The sun was up; she'd overslept. She grimly threw her kit together and met the crew downstairs, said little at breakfast, and wedged herself next to Grandma and her pile of pillows once again. Grandma seemed extra spunky, giving the bodyguards hell for rushing her, then giving them hell for the late start they were making.

The road through the hills from Cullman to Huntsville was so degraded that they crept along at a snail's pace. They got lost once, and had to back precariously down a switchback dirt road that had disappeared at the crest of a ridgeline. An infected subject crept after them on limb stumps, and each vehicle backed, crunching, over it. But otherwise, they made it all the way to Huntsville without incident.

They approached the gate late in the afternoon.

Vivian looked on in awe. This compound had the same double fences she was used to, but they stretched out of sight in both directions. The town itself was nothing but squat cement-block buildings surrounded by refugee camps, but the camps went on for miles, semi-cylindrical metal buildings that grandma called quonsets. Narrow roads defined the rows, corn and vegetable patches the columns.

Inside, Vivian supervised the hand-off of crates of precious vaccine to the town's chief doctor, Michael Franklin, who they called their "medical officer."

Afterwards, Vivian, Michael, and Grandma sat on wood folding chairs on the edge of the clinic's loading dock with a panoramic view of the grounds. They sipped lemonade spiked with fruit wine as afternoon grayed to evening. The whole polity was regimented. A horn blew for mealtimes, bath time, and bedtime. People used the facilities in shifts, and everyone knew their time to eat and bathe in the communal dining and bath halls.

"It's because it was a military base," Grandma explained. Seeing her granddaughter's quizzical expression, "The military was the way people massed together to kill people from other countries."

"I know that. That's something from before, that never made sense to me. Why did they want to kill other normal humans, when they all had plenty for everyone to live on?"

"Well, they didn't want to, not really. But someone could always convince them that different people were trying to hurt them, take their land, or ruin their way of life, so they had to hurt the others first."

"Sounds like mass insanity to me."

A hint of a smile. "Maybe it was, Vivian. Maybe it was. Certainly, the folks who couldn't drop their grudges, didn't survive very long when the real trouble hit."

Michael, a taciturn, angular man, had loosened up with the alcohol. He spoke up, "'Plenty' is a subjective term. It may seem to you that people before the Outbreak were rich beyond anyone's wildest dreams, but humans tend to only see what others have that they don't. Have you noticed the way the quonsets are divided up?"

"What do you mean?"

"This nearest one," he nodded, "is all Spanish-speaking."

"I noticed them talking as they walked by a little while ago."

"And that one," he lifted a finger, "is all male homosexuals."

Vivian smiled. "I did think it was odd that they were all men, and most of them so neatly groomed."

"The one beyond is all Christian fundamentalists. Pentecostalists, mostly."

"What's a Pentecostalist?"

"It's a religion that believes the Holy Spirit descends on the heads of true believers in tongues of fire. They shake and speak in tongues. Sometimes they fall down." Grandma interrupted.

"We didn't have any Pentecostalist churches around Eufala. There were some Holy Rollers at Cullman, you just didn't see them. They keep to themselves. The women cover themselves, keep their eyes down, don't cut their hair, don't wear makeup."

Michael snorted. "Religious fanatics. Anyway, the base commander found it simplest to put different groups in different housing assignments to cut down on conflict among them. But also, the people seem to prefer it because they can negotiate with the operations and logistics supervisors more easily for their group's specific needs."

The party was escorted to the main building and shown to spartan bedrooms. Vivian again shared a room with Grandma.

She was glad when they were finally alone, because it gave her a chance to fire off the questions only Grandma could answer: Could Carrie talk at all? (No). Did she know she'd given birth to Vivian? (She cared for her instinctively, like a cat with a kitten). What was she like? (She liked music, even sang a little. She had a beautiful laugh which would peal out, sometimes, for no reason. She slapped her forehead when excited, and Grandma mimicked her, slapping her forehead and trailing the palm of her hand down her face, over and over).

Vivian's dream that night was one of those rare, powerfully numinous dreams. The dream started as she drifted off to sleep, secure in her tableau of memory of her mother's gentle lullaby, and then segued backwards in time, in the crazy logic of dreams, into her mother's escape, Vivian now still inside her, a secret growing amidst the chaotic landscape of global catastrophe.

Dream time continued in reverse, and baby Vivian shrunk smaller and smaller until she vanished. Freed from embodiment, her perspective in the dream ascended to a historical sweep: The past glorious era of human ascendancy (which she might, no, which she would restore). Amongst that abundance, brutality: living, breathing humans taking each other's lives. And what's more, wrenching the gift of giving life from their own bodies and those of others.

She was breathless with the beauty of the technology and the burgeoning populace sparkling over the entire world, crowding out the plants and the beasts and the elegant, intricate, oblivious scheme of the ecology.

Abruptly, the dream time began to run forward again, but she remained in her god's-eye view: the darkness of the virus exploding across the panorama of humanity. Following behind its engulfing wave, the birds and fish and bugs and flowers and mosses and trees crowding in, reclaiming their lost domains. It was almost like the world breathing, this explosion and contraction of human life, a garish glitter on the face of the world which would in time, with the vaccine, reassert itself as inevitably as a dropped glass will hit the floor.

* * *

Vivian woke with quiet joy, sunlight still faintly pink with dawn streaming in the window of her private room in the base's main building. Today was the award ceremony.

She bathed and dressed in her finest dress, white cotton with lacy hand embroidery. The dream's impression lingered, pervading her mood and awareness with brightness.

An adjutant brought her and Grandma Emma a tray of breakfast, but they both ate sparingly.

He then escorted them outside, where she met her crew from Eufala, all spiffed up just like she was. They all fell in behind her, standing straight and proud as they entered the huge central parade ground and approached the stage.

A crowd was already assembling, funneled into the square using barricades, and down one side a long line of people stretched. A few relaxed MPs policed the line, keeping it moving smoothly. At the front were three tables. Each held a stack of vaccine ampules, a nurse at each one, administering shot after shot. Vivian beamed.

Just as the group reached the steps at the foot of the dais, a disturbance broke out at one of the tables. A woman with the long hair and skirts of a Pentecostalist, with eight children whizzing like electrons, she their nucleus, was raising a fuss.

"My brother and sister both died after having vaccines! They turned blue and foamed at the mouth and couldn't breathe. My mom said it was horrible the way they died! Horrible! I'm not vaccinated and none of my kids will be vaccinated either!" The children now clustered together, stairsteps, each a year or two apart in age from the next eldest.

The nurse tried to calm the distraught woman. "Maybe they had some other disease? A lot of the time completely different illnesses happen at the same time by coincidence and they get blamed on the vaccine."

"I'm not taking that chance! These kids are my life!"

Another mom nearby spoke up, "Everyone has to be vaccinated to produce herd immunity. I don't want your kids spreading disease to mine!"

The woman waxed aggressive and irrational. As she got louder and louder, the police who were maintaining order all migrated to the head of the line and to her table. She whipped her head around, frantic, when they surrounded her and separated her from the kids. Vivian could see their aggression was misplaced—someone had to defuse the situation

"Stay here, Gramma," she told Emma. She slipped out of her protective formation (to her escorts' dismay) and wedged herself into the fracas.

As Vivian moved in, she assessed the family. She noted that the woman's oldest child was a girl, a teenager. She moved a certain way so her belly strained against the long, loose dress she wore, and Vivian saw the girl was pregnant: perhaps six or seven months along. There were no men with the family group, and the youngest sibling was about four. The screaming woman was a widow, perhaps, or a single mother. And about to be a grandmother at about forty, not much older than Vivian herself.

Vivian slid past the last MP, putting a gentle hand on the woman's arm. The mother rounded on her, face crazed, aware of nothing, an animal defending her family. Vivian felt a jolt of raw panic at her snarl, and the nails that rose towards her face like daggers.

Before she could react, a pair of tanned, tattooed hands seized the mother's wrists. Following the hands to wrists, arms, shoulders, and a bearded face, familiar and protective, Viv recognized Zane, and her heart pounded its gratitude. His steady grip was strong enough to immobilize the attacking hands without hurting the mother.

Thus restrained, the mother paused, her chest still heaving with the residue of rage, long enough to take in Vivian's face and garb. She eased her struggling. The rest of Vivian's honor guard came bulling through the crowd, trailing the surprisingly agile Zane. They stopped short when they saw the situation under control. The mother fell silent, starstruck, her habitual meekness re-asserting itself. She twisted to look submissively at Zane, and he cautiously released her wrists, eyes locked with hers, ready to grab her again if necessary.

"What's your name?" asked Vivian softly. She turned from Zane to Vivian, the soul of gentleness now.

"Martha."

"Martha, do you know who I am?"

"Yes. You're the lady doctor who made the vaccine to stop the zombie sickness." "That's right. I made it so that you, your children, and your grandchildren-to-be," she cut her eyes towards the pregnant teen, "will be safe from the disease which has been killing us all for the last thirty-three years. I've taken it, my grandmother's taken it, and all the people near my home have taken it. Eufala now has half the—" *use relatable vocabulary*, "deaders we had a few months ago, and the few that're left are falling apart on their feet. People get bitten and don't convert.

"Martha, I can't tell you how important it is that this vaccine *works*! But: it can only work if everyone takes it. Listen: now isn't the time to be timid, Martha." Trying to build rapport with her patient, she let her voice echo the rhythmic cadence of a charismatic preacher. "*Now* is not the time to listen to some *scary* story your parents *told* you to frighten you as a *child*. You *need* to do what's right as a *mother*, and give yourself and your family the *best* chance to survive and be *safe*, and keep everyone else *safe*, too." She swept her hand in a stately gesture at the circle of spectators, including the cops (who'd stepped back a crucial half-pace, Vivian was grateful to see).

Vivian placed her hand on her own heart, dropped her voice to almost a whisper. "I swear to you, this vaccine is perfectly safe."

Martha searched Vivian's eyes. Vivian saw hope in Martha's.

After a few timeless moments, Martha turned to the nurse. She gave one short nod. "Okay," she said. "Okay, we'll do it."

The nurse didn't have to be told twice. Before the words were out of Martha's mouth, a syringe full of clear liquid jabbed her arm. The other two nurses stepped up to help, and all eight of the children got their shots as well, followed by a cheerful, tiny bandage. Martha smiled and picked up the youngest, a towheaded girl, still bawling from the needle stick. She stroked her blond curls. "That wasn't so bad now, was it?" The girl quieted to an intermittent, tragic sniffle, inspecting her bandage.

Martha grinned shyly at Vivian. "That truly wasn't so bad! I don't know what I was so worried about!"

Vivian nodded warmly, patted Martha's (unbruised, *Zane was so gentle*) forearm, and made her way back to the stage. She found her seat behind the podium.

She scanned the crowd and found Martha and her brood, who had filed in to fill the fourth row. Knowing those sweet children would never be infected, never turn into zombies, gave her a warm glow inside. *This is what makes being a doctor so rewarding. The one-on-one with patients, a firm hand and reassurance, when superstition and misinformation has made them afraid.*

She tried to catch Martha's eye, but Martha was wiping the baby's nose. No, the baby was falling asleep and she was trying to wake her up.

No, the baby was unconscious! The pregnant teenager was at the other end of the row, and she leaned precariously forward trying to see what was wrong. Then she tipped forward off her chair onto her knees, grabbing the back of the folding chair in front of her. The person in that chair turned in annoyance, and for a flashing moment, Vivian saw the pregnant teenager's face, turning a mottled purple. The other children went down like a row of dominos. The dark-haired boy, nine or ten, was having a classic grand mal seizure, flailing arms and legs, kicking and writhing as those around him tried to hold him still or tried to get away, everyone entangled with the folding chairs.

Vivian stood up, intending to descend the steps and administer first aid to the family, but her guardians blocked her. "Too dangerous," Zane said. She abided, impotent, confused, torn. The ethereal sensation of the dream had turned grim, and Vivian felt frustrated in her physician's need: to act, in order to push away the horror of the moment.

A vehicle with a red cross pulled up and four strong medics forced their way through the crowd to carry the family off.

Vivian found her voice. She insisted Zane escort her to the infirmary, ignoring the disruption of the planned ceremony.

She found herself clinging to his arm all the way there, desperate as a drowning woman clinging to a life ring.

Every physician makes mistakes, and sometimes things go wrong with patients for no reason at all. Ralph had taught her that and she'd learned to accept it years ago, learned to release guilt and what-ifs and remain dispassionate, move ahead.

Once they reached the clinic building, Zane hesitated. Vivian dropped his arm and walked alone through the ambulance-bay doors. The scene was bedlam. Every medical person on the base must have been at the parade grounds and instantly mobilized for this emergency. This tiny ER was used to treating zombie bites (amputation, or quarantine until euthanasia), but was taxed by dealing with seven children, of different ages, all at once. The medical team, stressed, were used to working together and it didn't even register with them that Vivian was a doctor.

The curly-headed toddler was sitting on mom's lap, an oxygen mask on her face, but awake, thank heaven! The boy with the seizure groaned, lolling on his side by a streak of his own vomit, batting away someone trying to shine a light in his eyes.

Vivian spotted the pregnant teenager on a gurney, half-in and half-out of a curtained bay, surrounded by scrub-clothed personnel, all scrambling to revive her.

"Blood pressure, 45/15."

"Pulse, flat."

"Anaphylaxis."

Someone tried futilely to start an IV in collapsed blood vessels. Someone was injecting epinephrine. More epinephrine. More!

Vivian had come to help, but there was nothing for her to do without stepping on someone's toes or getting in the way of the team trying to resuscitate the girl.

Light took on a brilliant clarity and every object was outlined vividly. She saw tiny details of every needle, wire, and connector. She saw the patient as the center of a sunburst of arms reaching towards her. She knew how the drama would end: life had left the girl for good.

Unaccustomed to standing still in a medical emergency, still processing the trauma of learning about her mother, she dissociated: she saw the whole scene as though from a birds-eye view. She was aware of the neat, precise lanes around it and the central square, where some still waited for the event, while others were leaving. She envisioned the entire compound, safe inside its protective fence. Outside, she saw the monsters, human bodies denied a clean death, changed into unwitting servants of the virus that had come so close to annihilating humanity.

Her vision telescoped back inwards: compound, hospital, room, girl. She knew what was going on inside the girl. Her doctor's mind envisioned the histamines flooding the patient's system, saw them trigger the cells of her throat to close, the muscles of her bronchioles to constrict, her blood vessels flaccidly lose their tone. She thought also of the tiny homunculus in her womb, thrashing quickly at first, and then more and more slowly, plummeting into dreamless sleep forever without ever being wholly awake.

Her perspective snapped back and forth, smaller and greater, faster and faster, until it became a vibration. The dead girl before her, her mother, her unborn child, strobed back and forth with the darkness of the virus battling the frenzied light of humanity across the face of the land, until the two images fused with her dream, and she saw it all.

Did Martha really choose? Did Carrie? Did anyone choose between humanity and nature?

* * *

The principle that sustains compulsory vaccination is broad enough to cover cutting the Fallopian tubes. Three generations of imbeciles are enough.

—Supreme Court Justice Oliver Wendell Holmes II, *Buck v. Bell*, 1927

* * *

This story first appeared in the After Dinner Conversation—July 2020 issue.

Discussion Questions

1. What do you think should happen with the new vaccine after the death of the family? What research, if any, should happen before the vaccine is used? What information would you want to know before releasing it?

2. Given that becoming a zombie is a pretty big deal, is there a % of acceptable vaccine deaths that would allow the vaccine to be released? 1% die? 5% die? 20% die? Does the severity of the sickness effect the acceptable death rate of the vaccine?

3. The story seems to argue against mandating vaccines as well as mandating sterilization. Is there a difference, if so, what is it? Would you be okay with mandatory sterilization for those who carry a gene that made getting the zombie virus more likely? Is there any acceptable scenario for mandatory vaccination or mandatory sterilization?

4. Is the ability to regulate what medicine you take *(or if you have children)* a "natural right?"

5. Is there an argument to be made that zombies are simply a new form of life, and *(like a lion)* have a right to feed and exist just like any other species?

* * *

Step Back

Henry McFarland

* * *

Beth never liked doctors' offices—the white sterile surfaces, the antiseptic smell, the degrees pretentiously hung on the wall. Bob's gently putting his hand on hers was comforting, but still she hated the waiting. Finally, Dr. Wilkins strode in, all brisk efficiency, and sat behind her desk. "Good news, Mrs. Stevens, your nausea doesn't stem from anything serious, you've conceived in utero—inside your body. That means—"

Beth's hands went to her belly. She had long dreamed of this. A child lived inside her! "That's wonderful!"

Bob reached over and hugged his wife. The two shared a long kiss before he spoke. "We hoped you'd say that—our first child."

"Excellent," the doctor's smile looked practiced. "I'm glad you're both pleased. Now it's a simple procedure to draw the embryo from where it's embedded in your uterus, and we can recommend some fine womb farms to nurture it until it's ready to go home as your child."

Beth had expected such nonsense. She'd dreamed of this moment for years and no one would ruin it for her. "Doctor we'll leave our child where she is. That's how people procreated for thousands of years, isn't it?"

A frown furrowed the dark skin of Dr. Wilkins' brow. "I wouldn't recommend that. The old method could lead to serious complications. Also, genetic enhancements are much harder in a natural womb—many are actually impossible."

Beth reminded herself to stay calm. "Complications are possible either way. I don't want those so-called enhancements—babies designed to look like everyone else, even babies without gender. Those aren't enhancements."

The doctor's voice sounded reproving, irritated. "I'm not suggesting that you do those things, but were a genetic illness to arise, we might not be able to deal with it in an internal pregnancy."

"Our families don't have a history of genetic illness, so I don't see why you raise the issue. Doctor, it's my choice, and I'm going to carry this baby the way nature intended."

Wilkins sighed in resignation. "Mrs. Stevens, this practice does not treat internal pregnancy. The only obstetrician still practicing that method around here is Dr. Pearson. I'll refer you to him."

Dr. Pearson could see them the next day. His office was on the lower level of an older building on the outskirts of downtown. Dust danced in the sunlight that streamed from the small windows near the ceiling, and his office had a musty smell, likely from the old medical books that filled the cases along the walls. That didn't matter to Beth. His shock of gray hair showed he had lots of experience, and she loved his manner. He gave her and Bob a big smile. "Mrs. Stevens is young and in superb health, an excellent candidate for internal pregnancy. It's great that you two won't mindlessly conform to how other people have babies today."

Beth was euphoric, a baby within her was all she wanted, and she knew the next few months would be great.

She watched her nutrition very carefully. Still she'd wake up with her stomach feeling queasy. Eating a few bland crackers helped sometimes, but other times she'd kneel next to the toilet and throw up. On a few days, the nausea lasted so long that she missed work. One day her supervisor called her to a conference room where a man from human resources waited.

Beth disliked the HR guy on sight. He looked cadaverous—skinny and pale as if he'd never been outside. He cleared his throat and started talking. "Ms. Stevens, your position requires a high degree of reliability, you have to be here when we need you. Because of the internal pregnancy, we can't count on you. Thus, we no longer require your services. Of course, we'll pay a two-week severance."

Beth called Bob at his work, told him of her firing, and shouted, "They can't do that to me! I'm going to find a lawyer and sue."

They set up an appointment with a lawyer, an older woman someone recommended. Her office was on one of the highest floors of a downtown skyscraper. She sat attentively behind a wide, empty desk as Beth told her story.

When Beth finished, the attorney cleared her throat. "I'm sorry, but I can't recommend that you bring a suit."

Beth couldn't believe it. "Firing someone for getting pregnant is illegal!"

"It was, Mrs. Stevens, but when internal pregnancy became rare, those laws were weakened. Your former employer can simply say your condition makes you unreliable, and unreliability is valid grounds for a discharge."

Beth sat there stunned. The lawyer went on. "It's not too late to switch to a womb farm—if you did that we might argue for your reinstatement."

Beth got up and walked out. Bob caught up to her at the elevator. He put his arms around Beth. "It'll be all right dear, we have my salary."

Beth leaned her body into his. Nothing would stop her from carrying the baby the way she'd planned.

* * *

Bob knew he should be nothing but happy—wonderful wife, child on the way. Still, Dr. Wilkins' talk of complications scared him. And while Beth seemed delighted with Dr. Pearson, Bob wondered why he took up space with paper copies of books that he could read on a pad. Plus, Pearson's thick glasses gave him an owlish look that didn't inspire Bob's confidence.

When Beth got fired, he told her not to worry. But how would they make it on only his income? They'd find a way—no more dinners out. He'd take a bag lunch to work and do more overtime. He'd make that be enough. Bob sometimes wondered why Beth was putting herself through that much trouble—nausea, job loss. But when he saw her patting her growing belly, he knew it was worth it to her. He would never tell her of his doubts.

It helped that they found a supportive friend. One day as Bob and Beth came back from a checkup with Dr. Pearson, they met two women waiting for the apartment house elevator. The younger one was short and skinny in a loose-fitting pink sweat suit. Her face was streaked with sweat, and her long brown hair was pulled back in a ponytail. She gave them a big smile. "Hi, I'm Sandy Moreschi. I just moved into 605." She nodded at the older woman, who smelled of soap and wore a high-necked white sweater under a brown jacket with a brown skirt that came to her ankles. "This is my mother. She's helping me move in."

"I'm Beth Stevens. This is my husband, Bob. We've lived in 908 for about a year."

Sandy's smile broadened. "It's a really nice building." Bob thought her voice sounded odd—not unpleasant but high and childlike.

As they all got in the elevator, the older woman stared at Beth's belly. "You look pregnant."

"I am."

"That's foolish of you, why don't you use a womb farm?"

Beth practically shouted her response. "Why, my womb works fine, why use a metal tank?"

Bob wished the elevator would go faster. He glanced at Sandy, who looked like she wanted that too. He noticed how pretty she was. Her eyes were wide but not deep set. Her chin was elfin, and her jaw was well-defined but light.

The older woman's voice grew stern. "For your information, womb farms have fewer risks than your old, outmoded way. Plus, you're throwing away the chance of genetic enhancements."

At the mention of enhancements, Sandy's jaw tightened, and her eyes narrowed. Bob wondered why. Beth stared at the older woman. "My child is not a science experiment! Mothers and children have bonded for centuries, by having the baby grow inside her mom."

The older woman's face turned red and her voice rose. "My child was conceived without the selfishness of lust and nurtured without foolish risks, and I love my child as much as you'll ever love yours."

Beth shouted back. "But you wouldn't let her be, would you? She wouldn't grow in you, it had to be a lab!" She sneered at the last word.

The elevator reached the sixth floor, and Sandy took her mother's arm and practically dragged her away. As the elevator doors were closing, they could hear the older woman from down the hall. "It's such a step back."

Just after dinner, Bob heard a knock on the door. Sandy stood there with a chocolate layer cake. "This is an apology cake—to make up for how rude my mother was today—two layers of devil's food with fudge icing."

Beth smiled. "You knew even internal pregnancy people love chocolate. Come on in."

Bob brewed coffee, and they sat around the dining room table talking and eating cake. Sandy asked if they were having a boy or a girl.

Beth shook her head. "We told our doctor not to tell us. She might be Elizabeth, or he might be Mark. I like naming children after their parents, Bob doesn't."

Sandy leaned closer to Beth. "A great custom, and so's internal pregnancy. I don't see why any woman who could have her baby grow inside her wouldn't do that." Bob heard a wistful note in her voice.

"It's definitely worth it, even if people don't understand." Beth told Sandy about her firing.

"That's awful. I can't believe they could get away with that."

"At least it gives me time to set up the nursery. It's lonely though. Bob's been working a lot of overtime lately."

Sandy's eyes widened. "I work from home four days out of five. Maybe we could do lunch sometime."

Bob was glad. Beth was alone so much lately with no work to go to and his long hours. Sandy would be good company.

* * *

Beth and Sandy's lunches together became frequent and often stretched far into the afternoon. One day it had already started getting dark as they walked back to their apartment building. A group of pre-teen boys stood on a street corner. A dirty faced kid in a baseball cap called out, "Hey, you so fat!"

They walked a little faster. The boys started to follow. Another yelled, "Why you hiding that baby? It ugly?"

Sandy turned to face them. "Leave her alone. It's not your business."

The tallest boy mimicked her, calling out in a fake high voice, "Leave her alone. It's not your business." Another boy yelled, "That's a freak, neuter, neuter, noooo terrrr."

Beth turned and pointed up the street. "See that cop car? Run home to your Mommas or they'll take you in." The boys scattered.

Sandy took a deep breath. "I'm glad you saw the cops."

Beth laughed. "What cops?"

Sandy looked up the empty street and laughed too, but she spoke no more until they reached their building. Then she took a deep breath. "Beth, maybe I should have told you before, but that boy was right. My body's asexual."

For a moment, Beth stared at her friend. Now she could see the asexuality. Sandy's body had no rounding at the breasts and hips. It wasn't a woman's body, more like a little girl who got tall. That was why Sandy always wore loose fitting clothes. Then Beth saw the uncertainty on her friend's face. "Come on, we can talk." The security system scanned Beth's iris and opened the building door. She led her friend upstairs.

When they got to Beth's apartment, she took out a bottle of brandy. "Want some? It'll help you calm down."

"Love some."

Beth poured a healthy dose of brandy into the glass and handed it to Sandy. "Sorry I can't join you. I found some pregnant lady advice on an old web site, and they say I shouldn't drink."

"I love how dedicated you are to carrying your baby."

"It's the way to go."

Bob got home and looked a bit surprised to see Sandy there. Beth handed him a glass of brandy. "Bob, Sandy wants to talk."

Sandy took a big swallow then began her story. "My parents are Neo-Shakers. They don't believe in having sex and think it's a great blessing that now you can have children without sex, and even without reproductive organs. They clone eggs and sperm. My parents had the womb farm delete some genes and block the expression of others, so I never developed those organs. They told me how lucky I was that they guaranteed my purity."

Beth remembered Sandy's mother, so cold and so self-righteous. She hugged Sandy. "It wasn't your fault."

Sandy's voice sounded small and lost. "They told me that

sexual organs can cause a lot of trouble—sexually transmitted diseases, unplanned conceptions. My grandmother died young of uterine cancer, even though she didn't have a genetic risk. They kept asking, 'Why have body parts you don't need but could cause a problem? The way you are is the next step in evolution.' To them it was all very logical. They wanted me to be pure and safe, like someone in a glass box who can be seen but not touched."

Sandy gulped down more brandy. She lifted her head and looked directly at them. The tone of her voice grew stronger. "I don't want to be an asexual. I always identified female, and I might be able to become more of a woman."

Beth put her hand on Sandy's arm. "How could you do that?"

"There's an operation that would give me a set of female sex organs. I'd still need a cloned egg and an artificial womb to have a baby, but I could have sex like other women. I need the insurance company to agree to pay for it. They haven't told me yet."

Bob got up from his chair. "Either way, you're always our friend. Can you stay for dinner? Only hamburgers, but the beef's natural, not synthetic."

For the first time that night, Sandy smiled. "You would have natural beef." She took a deep breath. "Knowing you two means so much."

Bob clinked his glass against Sandy's. "Here's to friendship."

Late that evening, Beth found Bob frowning at his pad. "What's up?"

"I googled the operation Sandy wants. They call it gender

assignment."

"Not our business, you know."

"Okay, but I'd never met an asexual before, and I was curious about the surgery. It's like the gender confirmation surgery they did for transsexuals, before they discovered how to prevent sexual dysphoria."

"Genetic engineering eliminating diversity again."

"But it's a lot harder. With gender confirmation, the patient's old sex organs could be used to make the new organs. With Sandy's surgery, they couldn't. It's painful and risky— some people even died."

Beth wished her husband worried less. "She needs it, Bob, to feel fully human, able to love another sexually. She has to do it."

* * *

Bob hated missing Beth's checkup, but he had to work. He was glad Sandy could go with her. When Bob got home, Beth met him at the door with a big kiss. "The appointment was great. The doc said everything is fine, didn't he Sandy?"

"He did say the pregnancy is progressing well." Sandy sounded tentative, and Bob thought she looked concerned. He knew he was. Beth had been getting a lot of bad headaches lately.

Beth walked over to the sofa. She moved very slowly. Not only was her belly enormous, but her ankles were swollen. She sat down, then brightened. "The baby's kicking me."

She pulled her sweater up, and they could see a protrusion from her belly—the baby's foot pressing against her womb. Bob reached out and felt his child's foot through his wife's body. He caught his breath at the thought of a new life.

Beth leaned back. "It's all worth it. It's so worth it."

Sandy invited Beth and Bob up for dinner the next day. Beth had a headache in the morning, and her ankle swelling worsened. She told Bob not to cancel, she was looking forward to it, but she leaned on him as he knocked on Sandy's door.

Bob responded to Sandy's perky hello with a forced smile. "I made chocolate mousse for dessert."

Sandy took the large bowl he carried. "Great, I'll put it in the refrigerator. Have a seat, the chicken and dumplings need a few more minutes."

Bob and Beth slowly moved over to Sandy's sofa. Before they could sit down, Beth's body shook. She cried out in pain and collapsed in Bob's arms.

Sandy ran back from the kitchen. "A share-car's downstairs."

With Bob on one side and Sandy on the other, they got Beth into the car. Sandy yelled, "Northside Hospital, it's an emergency, hurry."

The car's mechanical voice responded. "This vehicle must obey all traffic laws. Should I call emergency services?"

"YES! NO! We can get her there faster ourselves. Start trip."

As the car started moving, Bob shouted into his phone. "Call Dr. Pearson!"

In a moment, they heard Pearson's voice. "Your call is very important to me. Please leave a number, so I can call you back."

"Emergency alert! This is Bob Stevens. My wife Beth is in pain, and we're taking her to Northside."

"The system will alert me immediately."

Sandy directed the car to the ambulance entrance and

ignored the robotic voice telling her to move on. Bob got Beth out of the car, and a nurse came with a wheelchair. The nurse told Sandy she could only stay if she were immediate family and to tell her car to move AT ONCE!

They put Beth on a bed in an alcove screened off by white curtains, stuck an IV line in her arm, and hooked her up to a machine that began to whirr and beep. A lot of numbers appeared on a screen—Bob didn't know what any of them meant. Two women in white coats came in. The older one said to the younger, "I haven't seen a pregnant woman since medical school, have you?"

The younger one shook her head and looked over at Bob. "Mr. Stevens, Dr. Pearson called. He'll be here in about 15 minutes."

A man in blue scrubs wheeled in another piece of equipment. "I finally found the fetal monitor." He pulled up Beth's sweater and attached two things to her belly. The strong and steady thump of the baby's heartbeat filled the space.

Older white coat said, "I want to bring her pressure down. Is labetalol safe in internal pregnancy?"

Younger white coat typed something into her pad. "No contraindications."

"OK, start at one milligram a minute in her IV and see what that does."

Bob could do nothing but hope that worked. Blue scrubs connected something to Beth's IV. Beth clutched her head and moaned in pain. Older white coat asked what painkillers were safe in internal pregnancy. Younger white coat held up her pad. "Not many that we have."

"Ok, try max on the acetaminophen."

Blue scrubs put something else in Beth's IV, and that seemed to help, but her breathing still sounded heavy and labored. She opened her eyes halfway. "Bob, you look all blurry."

"Doctor Pearson is coming dear, you'll be fine."

"I can hear the baby's heart."

"It sounds really strong, doesn't it? Rest now. Don't worry. They'll take care of you, you and the baby."

She closed her eyes and didn't open them again. Bob heard the baby's heart slowing. A loudspeaker said, "Code blue, bay 5," and blue scrubs came in with younger white coat, who was staring at her pad. "Turn her on her left side and put her on oxygen, 10 LPM to start."

Beth didn't respond as blue scrubs turned her body and put an oxygen mask over her face. The baby's heart beat faster, but not as fast as before. They left Bob alone with Beth again. He was covered in a cold sweat. She stayed on her side, motionless and silent.

In about an hour, Dr. Pearson came in and nodded to Bob. He looked at the screen, then walked around the bed staring at Beth. He stepped out for a minute, and Bob could see him in the corridor conferring with the two white coats. Pearson came back with blue scrubs. "Mr. Stevens, unfortunately your wife needs an emergency C-section. We'll do everything we can for her. The nurse will show you where you can wait."

Blue scrubs led Bob to a waiting room, where he sat and stared at the clock on the wall. Why hadn't he insisted that Beth have the baby the usual way, not risk an internal pregnancy? What would his failure cost her? Cost their child?

Bob sat with his guilt and fear for hours until blue scrubs

came back. "Sir, you have a daughter. Come see her."

He led Bob down a long corridor to a room with a small bed where a tiny baby lay adrift in a sea of white linen. Beneath her little pink knit hat, he could see a tiny nose and chin that looked just like Beth's. "May I pick her up?"

"Soon sir, but you'd better come with me now."

They walked a short distance down the corridor to a large room where Beth lay hooked up to a lot of machines one of which slowly beeped. Bob quickly went over to her bed. Beth looked so pale, as if everything had drained from her.

Doctor Pearson and older white scrubs stood on the other side of the bed. Pearson didn't look Bob in the eyes. "Mr. Stevens, your wife developed eclampsia. It's a rare complication, very few women have it, but it's very serious—very hard..."

Older white scrubs spoke up. "I'm Doctor Jennings, we met in the emergency room. I'm very sorry, but your wife's heart stopped several times during the birth, and before we could restart it, she suffered severe irreversible brain damage. She can never awaken from this coma, and I have to recommend we withdraw life support." Jennings paused for a long minute, as if waiting for something. "Dr. Pearson agrees with this recommendation." Pearson just nodded.

Bob reached out and touched his wife's shoulder. "I saw our daughter, Beth. She's beautiful. A beautiful little girl, looks just like you." Beth made no response, but maybe she'd heard him. Bob began to sob. "Turn it off."

Jennings threw a few switches. The beeping slowed and finally stopped.

Bob couldn't call the baby Elizabeth—he named her Angela, his little angel. At home, he watched her sleep in her crib, so peaceful and innocent. She'd never know her mother, but she'd always have him. He brokenly called Beth's parents and his own. He kept the calls short—he couldn't deal with their pain now. Then he went through the apartment taking Beth's pictures and throwing them in a drawer. "You stupid, stupid, stupid fool! Why couldn't you have a baby like everyone else? You knew the risks! Why did you have to have it your way?"

The doorbell rang. Sandy stood there holding a pie plate. "Bob, I'm so sorry, I called the doctor's office, and the receptionist wasn't supposed to tell me anything, but she started to cry, and she told me, and we'll miss Beth so, and I made a quiche, so you wouldn't have to cook, because you have to take care of the baby, I put ham in it, it's a quiche Lorraine, I'm so sorry..." She broke into tears. Bob hugged her, and they both clung together until they heard another cry. It was time to feed Angela.

* * *

At the funeral home, Beth looked peaceful and still in her casket. Bob stood a few feet away from her, dreading that someone would ask him why he'd let her risk internal pregnancy.

Sandy was the first friend to arrive. Bob introduced her to his mother-in-law as Beth's closest friend. Sandy expressed regrets then went over to pray by the casket. Beth's mother whispered, "Beth told me about her. She's a neuter, isn't she? Or should I say they?"

"Sandy prefers she, and the better term is asexual."

"Still it seems odd she'd have a friend like that, given how Beth liked things natural."

"Beth wouldn't hold how someone was born against

them."

"Some say that's the next step in evolution—eventually everyone will be like that. Maybe they're right. Hard to say things should be natural the way it worked for Beth."

"Sandy doesn't think that way."

"I suppose." She looked at her daughter's casket. "If only you and Beth had used a womb farm. Before you were married, I told her I used one when she was born. Even back then almost everyone did. She got so mad that I didn't bring it up again. I should have." Her words tore at Bob. Wasn't he the one who should have insisted on a safer pregnancy?

Beth's mother walked off to greet some distant cousins, and Sandy came close enough to Bob that their sleeves touched. "Bob, you loved Beth, you respected her choices, and that was the right thing to do." Hearing that helped, but he still wondered if he should have done something that would have saved Beth.

Bob got a month of paternity leave, and Sandy visited him every day. She joined them when Bob strapped on a baby carrier and took Angela for her first outing—a trip to the grocery store.

Bob stared for a minute at a carton of synthetic breast milk before putting it in his cart. Sandy touched his arm. "You're thinking of how Beth planned to make her own, aren't you?"

"She was proud of that, no synthetics for our baby. But they've shown it's just as good. Some people even drink it themselves instead of cow's milk. Not me."

Angela waved her little arms and gurgled. Sandy stroked her cheek. "She looks great. She's doing fine on the synthetics."

When Bob went back to work, he put Angela in infant care. Sandy visited in the evenings. Angela's grandparents lived far way, so Bob was glad to have someone to share his delight in his daughter's growth. Sandy would lift Angela high in the air. "How's my favorite baby?"

The baby smiled and gurgled happily, and Sandy smiled back. "You're doing a wonderful job with Angela, Bob. See how happy she looks."

One evening, Sandy came in radiating happiness and carrying a bottle of champagne. "Great news! The insurance company will pay for my operation. Let's celebrate!" She popped the cork, poured two glasses, and proposed a toast. "Here's to the new me."

Bob clinked his glass against hers. Sandy kept talking rapidly. "Before they can do the surgery, they have to prep me with hormones for 14 months. I hate having to wait that long, but no choice. They'll actually perform the operation at Hopkins in Baltimore. It'll take about 10 days." She paused for a minute to catch her breath.

He remembered what he'd read about the risks of the procedure. Still, joy lit Sandy's face—he hugged her. "So happy for you, Sandy. You wanted it so much."

She went on excitedly talking about the treatment. Bob watched bubbles float to the surface of his glass and pop.

The next day they put Angela in a stroller and took a walk in the park. Sandy breathed deeply to fill her lungs with the crisp fall air. "Look at those trees, such beautiful reds and yellows."

Bob's hands were tight on the stroller. "Winter soon."

Sandy ran one of her hands over his. "Why so quiet?"

"The hormone therapy they'll give you can have side effects, like blood clots."

Sandy laughed then grabbed the brim of Bob's baseball

cap and pulled it over his eyes. "No worries Bob. I get tests for that. They'll be lots of effects, but they'll be good ones."

Her happiness made him forget his worries, for a while.

Over the next few months, the hormones slowly changed Sandy. Her hair got fuller, her face filled out, and her hips widened.

Angela changed even faster. Bob called Sandy one day. "We want to show you something. Come up for dinner tonight."

"Great, I'll bring a sweet potato pie for dessert."

When Sandy arrived, Bob threw the door wide open to show Angela standing with just one hand on the sofa for support.

Sandy handed Bob the pie and clapped. "Look who's standing up!" She went over and hugged Angela, who laughed in delight.

After dinner, Bob put Angela to bed then returned to see Sandy standing sideways to a mirror looking at her body in silhouette. "Do you think I'm getting boobs?"

"No doubt, yeah."

"They tell me because the hormones started later in life, they'll stay small. Think I should get them enlarged?" Bob put a hand on her shoulder and turned her to face him. "You'll be beautiful either way."

They kissed, then she backed up a step and put her forefinger to his lips. "Not ready yet."

Bob wanted to ask Sandy to always eat dinner with him. He needed another adult to talk to. But how would she respond? Then the day Angela took her first independent steps, Sandy asked, "Do you think we should share dinners every night? We could split the cooking."

"Great idea. Let's."

Dinner was always at Bob's to make it easier to put Angela to bed. Bob loved having someone he could talk to at every dinner. And Angela was always happy to see Sandy arrive. Her first word was "Da-Da" and her second was "San-San."

One night as they tidied up in the kitchen after Angela went to bed, Sandy said, "Bob, hormone therapy is almost over, and I have to meet with a doctor about the surgery. I'd like someone to go with me. Could you do that?"

Bob thought again about all the risks of surgery. He tried to keep the uncertainty out of his voice. "Sure Sandy, I'll come with you."

* * *

Dr. Dalbert's office had none of the old books or musty odor Bob remembered from Dr. Pearson. The doctor sat behind a large desk, his profile turned to Bob and Sandy, as he read data from a screen. Finally he turned to them. "Ms. Moreschi, tests found no reason not to go ahead with the surgery. Still you need to understand that the operation has the risk of serious complications. Also it's quite painful. We'll give you pain blocks of course, but they will only be partially effective. You'll be off your feet for 10 days minimum."

She nodded. "I understand."

"Before proceeding, we need you to sign our informed consent form, please read it carefully and ask me if you have any questions." He pushed a pad towards Sandy.

Bob asked if he could see a copy. The doctor looked surprised. "Is that all right with you, Ms. Moreschi?"

"Sure."

Bob took a second pad from the doctor and read about all the things that might go wrong: nerve damage, urinary tract blockage, sepsis, death. He heard Sandy saying she'd sign.

Bob grabbed her arm. "Wait, stop! It says you could die."

"I know that Bob, but it's rare."

The doctor spoke up. "There have been some deaths from this procedure, and the risk is never zero. But Ms. Moreschi is young and in fine health, an excellent candidate for…"

"That's what they said about Beth!"

Sandy asked the doctor to leave the two off them alone for a minute. Once Dalbert left, Bob took a deep breath. "Sandy, please don't risk it. What you are is so great. You don't need to be anything else."

"You're starting to sound like my mother, 'Why risk everything, you're taking a step backward'. She can't understand, but I want you to."

"I don't want to lose you too."

"The way you lost Beth?"

"She took a step back, and it killed her. You mean so much to me now."

Sandy reached over and took his hand. "Bob, I have to do this. I need to be able to love and be loved the way women can, the way they have since forever."

"Beth wanted to do things the way women had before— the way women had babies."

"And she took a risk, and she wouldn't have been Beth if she hadn't. I won't be me if I don't take this one. You respected Beth's choice. Please respect mine."

He could see the yearning in her eyes. "But you mean so much to me—so much to Angela too. Can't you see her smile when she sees you? You're loved now, Sandy, not sexually, but you're loved."

"I understand, and you and Angela mean a lot to me too. But I need to be made love to—to feel a man within me. This operation is the only way that can happen."

"I know you want that, Sandy, and I'd like to be that man. But it's not worth risking your life. Having you safe means so much more."

She gave a little half smile. "I'd like you to be that man too, Bob. I hope you will be soon. But there's no life without risk. I've got to try."

Bob realized he had no choice but to accept her decision. His arms trembled as he put them around her. "After the operation, come back to me."

She leaned into his body and returned his embrace. "I will."

He held her tight and hoped some of her courage would flow into him.

* * *

This story first appeared in the After Dinner Conversation—June 2021 issue.

Discussion Questions

1. Do you agree with Beth's choice to forgo science and carry her child naturally? Do you support Sandy's decision to use science to change the way she was born? What, if any, is the distinction between the two?

2. Is it wrong for science to alter a natural process like childbirth? How is the example in the story different than an incubation chamber for babies born premature? Would you fault Beth for refusing to allow her baby access to an incubation chamber?

3. Is Sandy's decision to be made female okay because it is using science to undo what her parents used science to do? Does it matter that the surgery will be a painful and risky? Does a person have an inalienable right to gender?

4. Sandy's parents were Neo-Shakers whose faith demanded the complete absence of sexual intercourse to be closer to God. Is their choice to make Sandy asexual different than child circumcision?

5. Should Bob have argued harder against his wife's choice to carry their child naturally, or Sandy's decision to become female? What, if anything, is the basis for his argument in each case?

*** * ***

All Harriet's Pieces

A. Katherine Black

* * *

Janie dropped the book into her lap and leaned her head against the outside of the translucent pig chamber. Warmth seeped from the chamber, a stark contrast to the cold atrium floor, covered with tiles Mama had found in some faraway place on one of her trips. Janie's wish to sink through the chamber wall, to find a way inside, was so familiar, it was almost comforting.

Harriet stirred. Standing on her four short legs, she side-stepped until her pig body leaned lengthwise against the inside of the wall, facing Janie. Harriet used her eyes, eyes exactly like Mama's, to look at Janie in a way that Mama never did. Never would. Her pig face tilted toward the book on Janie's lap. The one Janie had been reading aloud until a minute ago. The one about the pig and the spider who become friends. Janie was nearing the end of it.

"I don't—" Janie said. She held back the rest of her words. As much as she loved that book, she couldn't bear to face the end. Not this time. Because the pig will survive in the book. Because real life is nothing like books.

A chime played in the hallway, followed by a recording of Mama's voice. "Bedtime, child." Janie ignored Mama's schedule. She touched the chamber wall next to Harriet's pink floppy ear, wishing she could reach it. She'd always thought Harriet would enjoy a good scratch behind the ear.

The chime continued, growing louder. Mama's digitized voice repeated, every three seconds. "Bedtime, child."

Harriet held Janie's gaze. Janie's chin quivered.

After numerous bedtime calls rang through the atrium, Hartie plowed out of the bushes in the far corner of the chamber, trotting at a pace that seemed too fast for a pig. Stopping just inches from Janie, on the other side of the wall, he stared at her with eyes identical to Janie's own.

Normally, Janie would have snapped at Hartie. He was always nagging her, even if she couldn't hear him through the one-way com. All she could muster tonight, though, was a single word. "Fine."

The alarm stopped in response to her verbal acknowledgment. Hartie nodded, apparently satisfied. He walked over to Harriet and plopped down next to her for the night. Harriet closed her eyes, as if this were just some regular evening, like any other. Harriet deserved to know what was about to happen, but Janie didn't know how to tell someone they were going to die.

Janie leaned into the com on the chamber wall and said good night before standing and dragging her feet toward her wing of the house.

She readied herself for bed. Cleaned her teeth and her

face, put on pajamas, thinking all the while about the pigs. To keep the day from ending, she decided to tidy up her library, returning books to their shelves. Twenty-three books later, there was nothing else to do.

She went to bed, twisting in her covers all night long, until birds chirped outside the window, warning her of the coming sunrise. Sounds of movement echoed from somewhere in the house. Doors and voices. Too soon. Mama had promised Janie she could say goodbye before the procedure, but it wasn't even light out.

Jumping out of bed, Janie made her way from her room to the service wing. Automatic lights sprung to life as she passed down the hall, but stopped when she entered the stairwell. She made her way in total darkness, conjuring a picture of Harriet's face in her mind, to ward off the monsters threatening to leap out of her imagination. No auto-lights in the basement, either. She crept toward the faint glow ahead, the space under the atrium, under the pig chamber. She'd lost count of how many times she'd tried to break into the lift that led to the pig chamber. But something was different this time. Workers were here. Workers with codes and keys. Workers who wanted to take Harriet away.

Crouched behind a corner, watching the institute workers fiddle with buttons at the wall panel, Janie gauged the distance between the lift and the service door that opened to the grounds outside. She could get Harriet and run. Hartie, too. It could work. With a diversion. She surveyed tubes and pipes hanging down from the ceiling under the enclosure, looking for ones she could reach. Ones that looked fragile.

The commotion began quickly, panel lights blinking and

people gathering around tubes. Barely able to avoid the glare of their flashlights, Janie slipped over to the lift. Her hand froze, poised over the only button, with an arrow pointing up. Memories flooded, of all the times she'd pressed it before, to no avail. She pushed again, jumping when the bell rang, looking back to the service people. They appeared not to hear it over the rush of air, or gas, escaping from broken tubes. The door opened, and she stepped inside.

The air in the chamber was warm and a little wet. It smelled like a garden after a heavy storm. Her bare feet stepped onto the grass floor, soft and pokey at the same time. No pigs were in sight. She tried calling Harriet, but only a whisper came out. Hartie peeked from the bushes. Leaves shook around his face, around his wide eyes.

Janie spoke fast. "Where's Harriet? We have to go. *Now.*" Hartie ran out from the bushes to stand in the middle of the chamber. "Hartie, *where is Harriet?*"

Nodding his head toward the lift, Hartie let out a sound. It was the first sound Janie had ever heard from a pig. A whimper, but not like an animal. Like a person. Janie shuddered.

She walked over to Hartie. He was about the same size as her, but thicker and bent. Kneeling before him, Janie looked in Hartie's eyes. They were the same ones she saw in the mirror every day, but she could barely make them out right then, behind his tears. She hadn't realized that pigs could cry.

Janie's head felt light, like a balloon. She let her rear hit the floor and she sat, looking at Hartie's face as it fell out of focus. Hartie stepped forward and nudged Janie, rubbed his cheek against hers. It was soft.

An alarm sounded around them. "Oxygen levels low in

pig chamber. Oxygen levels low in pig chamber." Barely able to keep her eyelids open, Janie finally gave in and let them drop.

* * *

She woke in her own bed. Her body felt like lead, like she held the gravity of the whole world under her skin. The smell of the chamber still hung in her nose, the alarm blaring in the back of her thoughts. Harriet was already gone. It was time to accompany Mama to the institute.

She thought about staying in bed, maybe forever, but routine grabbed hold. She got up. Shower, clothes, teeth, hair. Until she stood at the threshold of her room, unmoving. Mama's voice rang through the speakers in her bedroom. "Breakfast, child." Janie couldn't tell if it was Mama's real voice, or the recorded one. Not that it mattered.

Her legs responded to the call as always, walking her through the doorway and around two corners, all the while her mind panicking at the impending pass through the atrium, through her most favorite spot in the world. The pig chamber came into view.

Only one pig stood on the other side of the wall, the exact age of Janie. With eyes identical to Janie's, lungs and kidneys and all sorts of innards exactly like Janie's, and with a heart that was breaking. Just like Janie's. She slowed as she passed Hartie. He stood beside the com, head bowed, eyes red. And then she broke into a run toward the kitchen.

Chimes rang through the halls after her, Mama's recorded voice saying, "Please walk, child," over and over. Janie continued her fervent pace, "Please walk, child," until she finally reached the kitchen doorway.

Mama sat at the breakfast table with her back to Janie,

cradling a coffee mug in both hands. A sob broke free from Janie's throat. Mama's head cocked slightly to the side, but she did not turn.

"Morning, child," she said.

Janie held the familiar distance between herself and Mama. She wanted to plead, to drop to her knees on the hard tile floor and ask that Harriet be spared. But there was no use. Mama wouldn't give her morning coffee to spare a pig. She surely wouldn't give her life to spare Harriet.

As if she could read Janie's thoughts, Mama said, "Harriet wouldn't have existed, if not for me." She sipped her coffee. "It was nice of you to entertain her, until she was needed. You'll understand some day."

She patted a hand on the table, next to Janie's waiting breakfast. "Before it's cold," was all she said.

Janie shuffled numbly. To the kitchen table, soon after from the kitchen to the car, and finally from the car to the institute.

Hours later, she sat with Uncle Lou in the family waiting area. It was a large room. Several clusters of soft furnishings surrounded tables ready to play videos, games, or the day's news. A few families huddled in spots across the room. Uncle Lou watched some politics show. Janie watched the other families, wondering what they had said to their pigs last night. Wondering if their pigs had known they were scheduled for murder this morning.

"Jane?" A hand rested on her shoulder. She scooted across the sofa, away from her uncle. "I've watched you read to that pig since before you could actually read." He chuckled. "It was hilarious, listening to the stories you made up when you were little, while you turned pages on some huge book. You imagined some of the most bizarre stuff, but you said it all so very matter-of-fact like, it made the craziness seem almost believable."

Janie remembered how she used to drag a pillow and blanket into the atrium and sleep against the warm chamber wall, while the pigs curled against the inside of the translucent barrier, as close to her as they could get.

"Jane, hon, I'm sorry you're losing a friend," he said. "But remember, you get to keep your mom. Without that spare heart inside her pig, your mom wouldn't have lived much longer."

Janie kept quiet. Uncle Lou would not appreciate the words wanting to burst from her mouth. She studied the other kids sitting with their families, wondered which of them read stories to their pigs.

Eventually a man in a white coat walked into the waiting area and over to Uncle Lou and Janie, to tell them news about the successful surgery. To inform them that the rest of the spare organs were in excellent condition, in deep freeze right there at the institute, waiting to be needed. Watching the man walk away and picturing Harriet pulled apart like a puzzle, Janie felt a tremor, deep in her guts. Like an earthquake that would never end.

* * *

Janie and Hartie sat together in the atrium a week later, separated only by the translucent wall. Janie had no book in her hand, and Hartie's pig face held no expectant look. A voice called from the direction of Mama's wing. Uncle Lou was summoning her to Mama's lounge.

"What took you so long?"

Janie stood at the double-door entry. Mama reclined on

her favorite chair, eyes closed. Janie could never tell when Mama was really sleeping.

"Sorry."

"I need to run to the office, only for a little while," Uncle Lou said, pulling on his sport coat. "Keep your mom company while I'm gone."

Janie didn't move.

"Come on. You don't have to do much. Just sit and hold her hand. The meds are keeping her quiet right now, anyway." Uncle Lou winked at Janie. They both knew how grumpy Mama could get when she was disturbed.

Like they'd so often done, Janie's legs responded to the adult command, while her mind protested. The cumulative effect was Janie walking awkwardly to the chair next to Mama and sitting down with an abrupt thud.

Uncle Lou yelled as he headed to the door, "Call me if you need anything."

And they were alone.

Mama's hand rested on the edge of the recliner. Janie brushed the tops of Mama's fingers before resting her hand lightly on top of Mama's. Mama's fingers were so cold, Janie wondered why they weren't blue. She thought that maybe cold skin only turns blue in books, but not in real life. Janie watched Mama's chest rise and fall with every breath, telling herself, *Harriet is in there.* Over and over. *Harriet is in there. Harriet is IN THERE.*

Such a strange thought, knowing Harriet had been taken apart. Dismantled, as the institute called it. Broken down like a lego toy. Harriet's heart went into Mama, and the rest of Harriet's Mama-parts went into some deep freezer. Eyes, lungs, kidneys, brain, and Janie wasn't even sure what other stuff. "We're the lucky ones, getting a pig when we're born," Mama had said so often when passing Janie in the atrium, reading to Harriet and Hartie. "You know, most people in this world can't afford their own pig."

Janie's teeth gritted. Tears slipped down her cheeks. Her hand pressed Mama's cold fingers, hard, then harder. Janie didn't care about cancers and diseases and defective organs, and she would surely never care about those things. She only cared about Harriet. She would run to the institute and break into the freezers and gather up all the pieces of Harriet, even tear the heart right out of Mama, if she only knew how to put them all together and make Harriet whole again. But she was old enough to know that wouldn't work, in real life. Real life was sickness and disease and murdered pigs.

If only Mama had a bunch more diseases, then all of Harriet's pieces would be almost put together again, inside Mama. If only Mama needed a new brain, then Harriet's brain would become Mama's. "They only take pieces of the brain," Mama said once.

The more pieces of Harriet, the better.

Janie stilled, looking at Mama as if she could see inside of her. Counting Mama's parts.

Mama twitched, and slowly opened her eyes. She moaned. "Child, I need a pill."

Janie removed her hand from atop Mama's, and straightened her back. She sat quietly, watching. Thinking. A few minutes passed before Mama stirred again. "Child," she said, louder. "My pills."

A calm washed over Janie. "Yes, Mama," she said. "Which

pill do you need?"

Mama smacked her lips. "I don't know, child. Call Lou. He'll tell you." She fell into deep breathing again.

Janie sat for several minutes, her mind calculating, and then she left the room.

She returned to the lounge with her arms full, walking through the doorway without hesitation. She pressed on Mama's arm. "Mama, wake up. You said you needed pills."

Mama attempted to open her eyes several times before she was successful. She focused on Janie's outstretched hand, cradling several colorful pills. "Are you sure these are the right ones?"

Janie lifted them to Mama's mouth. "Yes, Mama. I am absolutely sure."

Mama took the pills with some effort and drank water before laying back in her recliner.

Janie laid one of her bedroom pillows against the back of her own chair, puffing it up before she settled into the seat next to Mama and opened a book. She began reading out loud.

Mama's eyelids grew heavy, almost closing, until suddenly, they opened wide. She turned her head with effort to stare at her daughter, who was already on page two of her favorite story.

* * *

This story first appeared in the After Dinner Conversation—April 2021 issue.

Discussion Questions

1. Why do you think the family kept their donor pig in a place they could see/access it? Is this about respect, foolishness, or something else?

2. Assuming this organ donation technology was possible, do you support the idea of an organ donor pig? Would you, personally, take a life-saving organ from a donor pig? What if the donor animal were a higher, or lower, order animal? What are your animal intelligence limits for organ donation? *(rat vs. gorilla)*

3. If the value of life is on a sliding scale, why is it that we, as humans, get to judge the criteria by which other animals are judged? Wouldn't our scale be inherently biased towards humans?

4. Would you accept a donor organ from a clone (or twin) that was kept in a coma its entire life?

5. Do you think the little girl meant to kill her mother? If so, why?

* * *

Author Information

Sacrificing Mercy & Step Back

Henry McFarland is an economist and part time short story writer living in Virginia. He likes to use fiction to explore how people deal with changes in technology, particularly those that lead to ethical conflicts or challenge our idea of what is a human. He has published stories in the Starship Sofa podcast, *Andromeda Spaceways*, and *Every Day Fiction*.

The Human Experience

Jared Cappel's prose has appeared or is set to appear in various publications including Idle Ink, Literally Stories, and City. River. Tree. When he's not writing, he enjoys creating digital art known for its abstract imagery and vibrant use of color. A lover of wordplay, he's ranked as one of the top 50 Scrabble players in North America. *fineartamerica.com/profiles/jared-cappel*

Euthanasia

Kelly Piner, Ph.D., is a Clinical Psychologist who in her free time, tends to feral cats and searches for Bigfoot in nearby forests. Her writing is inspired by Rod Serling's *Twilight Zone*. Ms. Piner's short stories have appeared in *Litro Magazine, Scarlet Leaf Review, The Last Girl's Club/Wicked News, Rebellion Lit Review, The Chamber Magazine, Drunken Pen Writing, Storgy Magazine, The Literary Hatchet, Weirdbook, Written Tales* and others. Her stories have also appeared in multiple anthologies.

In Defense of The Harvest

Rebecca Christophi, an adventurer and mom, writes short stories, and has been published in *The Fredricksburg Literary and Art Review* and "Change: A Space Coast Writers Anthology." She is an MA candidate in Literature and Creative Writing at the Harvard Extension School. She is currently working on her debut novel *Doctors' Wives.* She resides in Florida with her husband, five children, and an overweight kitty.

Two-Percenters

CJ Erick stumbled into Dallas in search of love, great sushi, and access to big box stores. Having found all three, he now inhabits the city with his wife and their two ponderous and entertaining black-and-tan hounds. When exhausted from the reckless adventure of engineering, he pens tales of the space frontier, gothic horror, the occasional steam-punk mystery, and other unbalanced visions from caffeine-deranged nightmares.

The Decay

Sierra Simopoulos is a Canadian writer who seeks to use her writing to make people think more deeply about ethical issues and moral tragedies that are often ignored by our society. She recently completed an English specialist at the University of Toronto which helped to develop her love of classic literature and good earl gray tea. She lives in Toronto with her wonderful husband, George.

Visions of Midwives

C.S. Griffel teaches English and Creative Writing at a small university in central Texas. Besides short stories, she writes screenplays and is learning to love poetry. Her stories also appear in the *William and Mary Review* and *Talon Review*. She is also published in "I Found Happiness and Tragedy: Selections from the 2022 Literary Taxidermy Competition."

On Good Authority

Peri Dwyer Worrell grew up white on a Puerto Rican street in New York, gaining a keen appreciation of the value of diversity, tolerance, and taking no crap from anyone. After thirty years as a physician, Peri became disabled and expatriated to Latin America. Peri writes fiction and poetry, and edits scientific articles.

All Harriet's Pieces

A. Katherine Black is an audiologist and a writer. She enjoys multicolored pens, stories featuring giant spiders, and nearly everything at 2am. She lives in a house surrounded by very tall and occasionally judgmental trees, along with her family, their cats, and her overused coffee machines. *flywithpigs.com*

Additional Information

Reviews

If you enjoyed reading these stories, please consider doing an online review. It's only a few seconds of your time, but it is very important in continuing the series. Good reviews mean higher rankings. Higher rankings mean more sales and a greater ability to release stories.

Print Books

https://www.afterdinnerconversation.com

Purchase our growing collection of print anthologies, "Best of," and themed print book collections. Available from our website, online bookstores, and by order from your local bookstore.

Podcast Discussions/Audiobooks

https://www.afterdinnerconversation.com/podcastlinks

Listen to our podcast discussions and audiobooks of After Dinner Conversation short stories on Apple, Spotify, or wherever podcasts are played. Or, if you prefer, watch the podcasts on our YouTube channel or download the .mp3 file directly from our website.

Patreon

https://www.patreon.com/afterdinnerconversation

Get early access to short stories and ad-free podcasts. New supporters also get a free digital copy of the anthology *After Dinner Conversation–Season One*. Support us on Patreon!

Book Clubs/Classrooms

https://www.afterdinnerconversation.com/book-club-downloads

After Dinner Conversation supports book clubs! Receive free short stories for your book club to read and discuss!

Social

Connect with us on Facebook, YouTube, Instagram, TikTok, Substack, and Twitter.